THE ANGEL OF DEATH

THE ANGEL OF DEATH

OF DEATH

a forensic mystery by
Alane Ferguson

SLEUTH
VIKING

VIKING
Published by Penguin Group
Penguin Group (USA) Inc., 345 Hudson Street, New York, New York 10014, U.S.A.
Penguin Group (Canada), 90 Eglinton Avenue East, Suite 700, Toronto, Ontario, Canada
M4P 2Y3 (a division of Pearson Penguin Canada Inc.)
Penguin Books Ltd, 80 Strand, London WC2R 0RL, England
Penguin Ireland, 25 St Stephen's Green, Dublin 2, Ireland
(a division of Penguin Books Ltd)
Penguin Group (Australia), 250 Camberwell Road, Camberwell, Victoria 3124, Australia
(a division of Pearson Australia Group Pty Ltd)
Penguin Books India Pvt Ltd, 11 Community Centre, Panchsheel Park, New Delhi –
110 017, India
Penguin Group (NZ), Cnr Airborne and Rosedale Roads, Albany, Auckland 1310,
New Zealand
(a division of Pearson New Zealand Ltd)
Penguin Books (South Africa) (Pty) Ltd, 24 Sturdee Avenue, Rosebank, Johannesburg
2196, South Africa

Penguin Books Ltd, Registered Offices: 80 Strand, London WC2R 0RL, England

First published in 2006 by Viking, a member of Penguin Group (USA) Inc.

10   9   8   7   6   5   4   3   2   1

LIBRARY OF CONGRESS CATALOGING-IN-PUBLICATION DATA IS AVAILABLE
ISBN 0-670-06055-0 (hardcover)

Printed in the U.S.A.   Set in Bookman ITC light   Book design by Jim Hoover

For George Nicholson — agent,
friend, and guide.

THE ANGEL OF DEATH.

Chapter One

"DO YOU KNOW how many laws we're breaking?" Cameryn Mahoney demanded.

Deputy Justin Crowley shrugged nonchalantly. He was driving his Blazer with one hand draped lazily over the wheel while the other brushed back his too-long dark hair from his eyes. "Well, if I had to guess, I'd say at least six," he answered slowly. A smile curled at the edge of his lips, making a kind of comma in his cheek as he added, "Maybe more."

"Six laws. And this doesn't worry you?"

Another shrug, only this time his shoulders barely moved. "Not particularly."

"*Why* does this not worry you?"

"Because there's a dead body on the side of the road, which can't stay there. That's a fact. The sheriff and the coroner are out of town, which is also a fact. That leaves the two of us—Silverton's trusty deputy and its extremely capable assistant to the coroner"—he nodded in her direction—"to work the scene. In other words, it's just you and me. And we're doing it."

"This is crazy. *You're* crazy."

"Just doing my job."

Trees whizzed past as Justin downshifted around a hairpin turn on the Million Dollar Highway, a narrow two-lane road that ran like an umbilical cord from tiny Silverton all the way to Durango. To Cameryn's right, Colorado's San Juan Mountains towered above her in a granite block, while to her left the mountains fell away in a thousand-foot sheer drop, a yawning mouth of a valley bristling with Engleman spruce beside streams with fluted ice as thin as parchment. According to Justin, there was a body on this road that Cameryn was supposed to process, without tools or a gurney or even a pair of latex gloves. Messing up at the beginning of a case could mean disaster if it ever went to court. They shouldn't even think of processing a scene alone. It was insanity.

"You're chewing your fingernails again," Justin pointed out. He glanced at her for the briefest second, and in the relative dimness of the car's interior his eyes looked more green than blue, the color of a lake reflecting evergreens. "What are you so nervous about? I thought you liked this stuff."

"I *like* being prepared and I—this—this is all wrong. We should radio the police in Durango or Montrose. Or something."

"*Relax.* You've been so uptight lately—did you know that?"

"We were talking about the remains, Justin, not about me."

"All right, all right, back to the case. There's something funky about the body. All I'm asking for is your quick, professional opinion and then . . . boom." He hit the heel of his hand against the steering wheel. "You're outta there."

The seat belt cut into her neck as she twisted to face him, protesting, "But I'm *not* a professional. How can I give a professional opinion when I'm still in high school?"

"Ah, but you've got to admit you know more than I do," Justin replied. "You're a forensic guru. You're so good that—guess what Sheriff Jacobs calls you when you're not around! Come on, take a guess."

Cameryn closed her eyes and groaned. She knew what was coming. A quip, a sly remark about her working with the dead—she knew folks in Silverton whispered about her all the time, under their breaths, their words falling like snowflakes only to melt beneath her resolve. It didn't take much time with the living to remind Cameryn why she wanted to be a forensic pathologist. The dead didn't tell stories, except about themselves.

Although Justin seemed to register her groan, there was no stopping him this morning. "Jacobs calls you the Angel of Death." The deputy grinned as though he'd just given her the highest compliment. "What do you think about that?"

She replied with her standard answer, the one she always gave, her Pavlovian response. "I'm into the science of forensics, not death."

"Tell it to the sheriff. *I'm* not the one who gave you the name." His eyebrows, dark half-moons, rose up his forehead as he smirked. "Angel."

Another hairpin turn, only this time a huge semitruck roared up the mountainside, belching greasy smoke into the morning air and leaving a gassy trail behind.

Like a vapor winding its way through the streets of Silverton, the idea that she loved death had dissipated throughout the tiny town of seven hundred citizens and had crept its way through the halls of Silverton High. It encompassed her friends, who squirmed at the fact that she'd seen the insides of a human body. It drifted over to her boss at the Grand Hotel, who made Cameryn soak her hands in bleach water before setting the tables, something he never asked the other servers to do. Her own grandmother, whom she called "Mammaw" after the Irish way, clucked whenever Cameryn read forensic books, convinced that the mere study of those books would somehow condemn her soul to hell. But her father, the real coroner of Silverton, encouraged her. "You've got a talent, Cammie," he'd say. "You *see* things. What you have is a gift."

The blinker's staccato clicking broke into her thoughts as Justin pulled onto a dirt overlook. He pointed expansively across the highway. "It's over there," he said, "behind that big boulder."

"You keep calling the body an 'it.' Is the decedent a male or female?"

"Hard to tell. Our little animal friends did quite a bit of chewing on it. That's not what's bothering me, though." He turned the key, and the engine coughed and died. "I think the best thing will be for you to see for yourself."

"I can't believe I'm doing this."

"Come on," he said. "Check it out."

Beyond the dirty windshield Cameryn saw a partial mound on the left side of the road, smaller than she'd expected, although the entire shape was impossible to discern from her angle. She got out of the Blazer and hurried behind the deputy as he crossed the highway. The lip of the road was narrow on the east side, the ground uneven, treacherous with rocks and roots. Beneath her, the faraway trees looked as though they were set in miniature. She slipped on a layer of faded leaves pooled at the trunk of a tree and made slick with melting frost, but Justin grabbed her elbow to steady her.

"Careful," he said.

Panic whined inside her because she knew she shouldn't be here. Maybe there was still time to call for help. . . .

"It's right there," Justin said, gesturing with his free hand.

Beyond the rock, rising like a half-shell, was a body, shadows dappling the surface of what looked to be the remains of a small person. The sickly sweet smell of decay filled her nostrils, but she ignored it as she moved closer, her heart drumming with nervous energy. Something was happening; it was as though a switch inside her had been thrown. Now the clinical side, the science part of her brain, pushed to the forefront, drowning out the objecting voices. Suddenly she wanted to see the body and examine it. There was a puzzle here, and it was possible she could put the pieces together to learn its secrets.

"I knew you'd get into it," Justin said.

"Uh-huh. Shut up."

Another step closer and she stopped in her tracks. The shape solidified in front of her, the mound a back that ended in a question mark of a tail. Tufts of fur bristled at the top of its ears, but the snout looked bent, like the crook in a branch.

"What is this?" she demanded, whirling around to face Justin. "You brought me out here to look at a *German shepherd*? You dragged me from work to look at *road-kill*?"

Rocking back on his heels, Justin returned her gaze. He was lanky, as tall as her father but much thinner. Hands in his back pockets, he said, "I never claimed the decedent was human."

"Oh, you are *so* hilarious," Cameryn snapped. She was relieved, of course, but, she had to admit, disappointed, too. Somewhere along the line she'd psyched herself up to see a human body. In the mountains, dead animals were a dime a dozen. "Why did you bring me here?"

Justin spoke as though he had all the time in the world. "I've discovered that in a small town, the deputy does all kinds of odd jobs. Dumping roadkill is one of them."

"Take me back, Deputy. I'm not a vet." Annoyed, Cameryn turned to leave. Justin caught her arm.

His voice became serious. "Just wait. The point is that when I saw the dog, right away I noticed there was something off about the body. I didn't want to dispose of it until I got a second opinion."

She began to pull herself free, but his grasp was firm. Then he gave her arm a squeeze, trying, it seemed, to cajole her. "Come on," he said, releasing her elbow. "You're already here, so you might as well look. Tell me what you see."

It occurred to Cameryn that, since Justin was driving, she really had no other way back, which translated to the fact that she had no choice but to examine the dead animal.

"Fine," she said at last. "I'll look. Then we go."

"Whatever you say. Angel."

"Punk."

Cameryn walked around the rock to get a better look at the carcass. Above her, the bare limbs of trees reached like scaffolding into the sky, creating a crisscross pattern of shadow on the rock and the body beneath. The dog's legs were already extended in rigor mortis, and its belly was distended. Fur stood in erratic tufts that reminded her of fish scales, and one ear was double-notched in a *V* as though it had been torn in a dogfight. A chunk of flesh was missing near its genitals. Wild animals had gnawed on the soft tissue, which was common in the mountains—nothing lasted in the outdoors, Cameryn knew. The tip of the German shepherd's nose, as well as its eyes, were missing, and the end of its tongue was gone.

"How long do you think it's been dead?" he asked.

"It's hard to say. From the rigor I'd guess about thirty-six hours. Maybe more."

Justin squatted. His elbows drilled his thighs; his hands hung limply between his knees. "Here," he said softly, pointing to the dog's head. "This is the reason I brought you. Do you see it?"

"You mean the eyes?" Crouching beside him, Cameryn studied the empty holes. "That could be from bird activity. Magpies are total scavengers."

"I thought of that. But look closer. It almost seems like

they, I don't know . . . exploded or something. Tell me if I'm crazy."

"You're crazy."

"I'm being serious, Cameryn. Say the word and I'll dump the carcass. But I really want your opinion before I do."

For a few moments she was silent, thinking. She bent close, only inches from the dog, breathing from her mouth to help fight the smell. The inside of the eye socket was exposed, and the vitreous humor—the transparent jelly that filled the eyeball—was missing. Ants had found their way into the orbs along with a few small beetles, which darted around the inner lid. A starburst pattern had seeped into the short hairs around the lids, giving it the appearance of painted lashes. The look was almost comical, and that fact alone made her sad.

"Have you ever seen this dog before?" Justin asked.

"No. My guess is that he belonged to someone who has a cabin in these mountains. It was a pet, though."

When Justin looked at her blankly, she added, "It was wearing a collar. See? The fur's pressed down around its neck in a ring. It must have worn a collar all its life."

"Then where's the collar now?"

Cameryn shrugged. "Who knows? There's no impact wound to speak of, at least on this side," she said, her gaze searching the ribs and abdomen. "By the way, it's a male."

"I can see that. Do you want to turn him over?"

"I would if I had my gloves."

"I've got a pair of work gloves in my Blazer." A moment later, Justin was back sporting thick leather gloves, as heavy as a falconer's gauntlet. He wore a green aviator-style jacket with the gold star emblazoned on the chest, which was regulation, although the faded jeans and cowboy boots were not. Grabbing the dog's back leg, he raised the stiff body. More beetles skittered out and disappeared into the nearby leaves. Although it was November, Cameryn knew insects worked year-round, drawn to the warmth of decomposing flesh.

Then something caught her eye: on the back side, Cameryn could see a place where the soft tissue had been ripped open by scavenger teeth.

"That's odd," she said. She picked up a stick and inserted it into the cut, separating the tissue from the bone. "See the muscle there? It's gray."

"From decomposition?" he asked.

"Maybe. I've just never seen decomp look like this before. The texture's off, too." She shook her head. "Weird."

"Do you think we should do an autopsy on it to see what happened?"

"If it's on an animal it's called a necropsy, and no," she said, rubbing her hands on her jeans as she stood. "I don't think we need to do one. I mean, the truth is, dogs die. Just like people. Things come, then they go, and then it's over—that's all there is."

For a beat he stared at her, releasing the dog's hind leg from his gloved hand. The carcass made a sickening thump on the ground. His eyes locked onto hers, and without flinching she returned his gaze.

"What?" she finally asked. "What's wrong?"

A pause, and then, "You."

"What about me?"

"I . . . I didn't think you'd turn like this. You've changed, Cameryn. You're not like yourself anymore."

She snorted. "You *are* crazy. I'm totally and completely fine."

"No, you're not." His green-blue eyes narrowed into crescents as he stood, towering over her. "The truth is, you haven't been fine ever since I gave you that letter from your mother."

The sound of his words was like a knife going through her, but she didn't move. She stood as stiff as the carcass on the ground.

Justin put his hand on her arm again, more gently this time. "You can talk to me about Hannah," he said. "Anytime you want."

"Are we done? Because I'd like to go now."

"You flinched when I said her name."

"Hannah is none of your business."

"It *is* my business. I'm the one who put the two of you together. If it weren't for me, you wouldn't even know she's alive. I feel responsible, that's all."

Her mother Hannah, who had been missing for years, had suddenly reemerged from the shadows like a phoenix rising from the ashes. Now everyone, it seemed, hovered over Cameryn, anxious to find out what was happening inside her head, as though they possessed a set of sharp autopsy instruments all their own, poised and ready to pick her mind and dissect her heart. But she wasn't willing to share what had happened with Hannah, especially not with Justin. Or with anyone. And so, in order to conceal her feelings, she hid behind the mask she had perfected for public scrutiny: rigidity without, hiding the storm within.

He took a step closer, near enough that she could smell the wintergreen on his breath. As she looked up, her dark hair fell down her back, almost to her waist, that waterfall of hair that she wished she could disappear inside. But there was no hiding this morning, not from Justin's sharp gaze.

"I'm your friend and I care about you, Cammie," he began. "You may not see what's happening, but I do."

"If you really cared you'd leave me alone."

She raised her chin and kept her eyes cold, folding emotion inside her with neat hospital corners, tucked under where no one could see. "You want my professional opinion?" she asked. "Here it is: The dog is dead. There's nothing you can do except make a note of it and move on."

Overhead, a magpie cawed. When Cameryn looked

up, she noticed that light snow had begun to fall. The snowflakes were sparse, dry, crystalline bits easily brushed away. Neither of them moved. One flake landed on Justin's cheek, another on his lashes. They rested on the dog's fur, too, creating the thinnest of shrouds. In a way she envied the dog, whose struggles were already done. Hers were only beginning.

Cold was seeping into her, past her jacket, through her pink sweatshirt and her running shoes, and into her toes.

"Are we done with the therapy session?" she asked. She attempted a smile, trying to soften things. Justin was only trying to help, after all. "I appreciate what you're trying to do. But I'm really okay. Really."

Justin seemed to know he was beaten. "Suit yourself," he finally said. "But if you change your mind, remember I'm here."

"Thanks. I'll remember."

Without another word, Justin reached down and picked up both the foreleg and the hind leg of the dog. He dragged the stiff carcass to a spot on the roadside where the trees had thinned. Then, with a mighty heave, he thrust the remains into the sky. The dog's carcass sailed in an arc, like a discus, before disappearing into the underbrush below.

It would be hidden now. Just like her secrets.

Chapter Two

"WHAT ARE YOU doing home so early—I thought you had work today!" Mammaw cried in surprise as Cameryn entered the Mahoney kitchen.

Cameryn slid into a chair and grabbed an apple from a green ceramic bowl. Then, thinking better of it, she let it roll back with the others. "Justin asked me to help him on a case, which turned out to be a dead dog, so when I got back to the Grand my boss said I should take the rest of the day off."

Her grandmother, as usual on a Saturday, was making bread. Mammaw slapped and punched the ball of dough beneath her flour-encrusted fingers as though she could somehow beat it into submission. Like the rest of Mammaw's compact body, her fingers were deceptively strong. "You left work for a dead dog?" she grunted.

Cameryn sighed. "It's a long story."

"Justin Crowley had no business taking you from the Grand. Your father will be home any minute, and one thing's for certain—he won't like hearing about this!"

"Then don't tell him."

Her grandmother didn't answer. Instead she made a *tsk*ing noise between her teeth as she punched the bread with the heel of her hand. The next words out of her mouth were the words Cameryn could always count on her to say, as rote as prayer. "Let me get you something to eat," Mammaw offered. "I've got some boxty in the refrigerator, and you're as thin as a sparrow."

"Maybe later."

Mammaw's lips were already compressed in disapproval as she murmured, "Do you see what looking at death does? It kills the appetite."

Although it had been nearly sixty years since Mammaw had lived in Dublin, the Old World still clung to her like the blue waves of incense Father John swung from his censer in church. A rosary clicked inside her apron pocket, and a picture of the pope smiled beneath magnets on the refrigerator. The cross that hung from her neck was Celtic, ringed with a halo, the symbol of which Mammaw claimed came from St. Patrick himself.

But somewhere along the way she'd become Americanized, too. Her snow-white hair had been cropped short, like a man's, and twice a year she made a trip to play the slots at The Lodge Casino in Black Hawk with other gray-haired ladies from St. Patrick's Catholic Church. On those occasions, with her thin lips painted in roseberry hue and a layer of powder on her nose, Mammaw looked just like any other Western woman bent on losing money.

"I ran into Velma today, and she told me the pictures for the yearbook are already due," Mammaw said now. "We'd better look into it. Lord above, I can't believe we're talking about your graduation already—where does the time go? Oh, and Father John says he needs your help a week from next," she went on in her soft Irish lilt. "I told him you'd call. Don't forget."

"I won't."

Cameryn looked at the row of flowers her grandmother had brought in from outside in order to nurse them through the winter, confined in their pots but secure from the elements. Cammie had always felt safe in this kitchen, in this house, in this life. Her grandmother was the only mother she had ever known, a woman as solid and rooted as Ireland's native alder trees.

Mammaw hesitated. "I'm not meaning to press, but I want to know if you're tense because of your mother."

"Mammaw!"

"No, no, hear me out. To have her burst into your life only to disappear again—well, it's a lot for anyone to bear.

Your father and I are worried. It's only been a month since you got the letter and—the nerve of the woman, begging you to call her on a telephone number that was no good. I can't help but think it's heavy on your mind."

"I already told you I'm over it, Mammaw. I called, Hannah's number was disconnected, and that's it. End of story."

"You're sure?"

"Yes."

Her mammaw smiled and shaped the dough. The news that Hannah had slipped away again confirmed everything Mammaw had always suspected about her daughter-in-law, and she'd wasted no time in telling Cameryn exactly what she thought. "I'm sorry for your pain, Cammie," she'd said. "But hard truths are better when you take them straight. Your mother *said* she wanted contact with you, but clearly she wasn't ready. And I have to admit I'm relieved. So's your father. It's a romantic thing, thinking about a lost mother rising up like the dead, but Cammie, Hannah's never been a well woman. It's better if she stays away. It really is."

With unerring instinct, Cameryn had surmised exactly what her father and grandmother wanted from her. They wanted her life—the lives of all three of them—to stay just as they were, to go on in their rhythms. There had been a shock, yes, but Hannah had disappeared once more and life could go on as it always had.

Yet when the call had come for Cameryn at the Grand Hotel and she had listened to her mother's breathy voice, she'd made a decision of her own. To give herself the time she needed to sort out everything, she would keep this new contact with Hannah a secret. The roles had been ironically reversed: now it was *Cameryn* who knew what her father and grandmother did *not* know. It wasn't payback, exactly. More like justice.

"What are you thinking about, girl? What's spinning inside that head?"

Cameryn looked up. She blinked, then said, "Nothing."

Her mammaw sighed. "All right. I can't reach in and pull out your thoughts. So while you're thinking about nothing, there's some laundry of yours that needs to be folded. I left the basket in your room. I also noticed your bed wasn't made."

Raising her hands in mock surrender, Cameryn cried, "Okay, okay, I'm going. Bed made, clothes folded. I got it."

"I'll make you something to eat when you're ready," Mammaw called as Cameryn hurried up the narrow stairway.

In her bedroom, her bed lay rumpled. It had once held a canopy, but she'd long ago taken off the top so that the bedposts stood bare, rising like steepled spires toward the ceiling. Leaping onto the middle of her bed on top of a mound of blankets, she began to fold her clothes, enjoying the small static sparks as she pulled her things apart. When she had a stack of underwear, she crossed over to her dresser and opened the drawer.

And there it was. Beneath the lacy bras, she saw the edge of a wooden picture frame, painted deep violet. She shoved the bras aside and lifted the picture.

The dreamy watercolor painting was evidence that her entire life had been built on a lie. That wasn't exactly right, but that was how she felt. Both her grandmother and her father had lied to her. Not the deliberate lies she'd learned about in church, those acts of commission, but rather an act of omission. The truth lay in the painting Cameryn held.

There they were, a pair of small, dark-haired girls in pink smocking, smiling the same shy smile, telling the same immutable truth she'd learned the night she'd read the letter from Hannah: Cameryn had once been a twin. Two halves of the same whole. Only the twin was gone, and Cameryn had been taken, borne away by her father to tiny, safe Silverton, where the San Juan Mountains would become the walls of her cloister.

Staring at the picture, she studied her sister's face. "How can I have no memory of you?" she whispered. "Little girl Jayne, lost and buried, gone forever. Why can't I remember?"

In her mirror she caught sight of her own reflection and suddenly understood the reason they were all becoming afraid for her. Her dark eyes, large in her face, had a hollowness that hadn't been there before. Leaning in, she studied them, only inches away. They looked haunted. Would her mother even recognize her now? There was little resemblance between the child in the painting and the mirror's reflection. Baby fat had melted away, and her face was longer, with high cheekbones and smooth lips. Yet her twin, frozen in time, would never age. "If you were here I wouldn't be alone," Cameryn murmured. And, for the millionth time, she wondered what might have been.

"Hey, beautiful one, whatcha doing? Admiring yourself again?"

Whirling around, Cameryn saw her best friend Lyric in the doorway.

"Could you knock or something?" Cameryn cried. "You almost scared me to death!"

"And why would a knock be less frightening? I say you would have jumped out of your skin either way."

Lyric had on a kinetic print of blues and reds, what she called a "3-D look"—the kind of pattern made with a paint wheel in school. Her pencil-leg jeans had been tucked into black boots with fringe along the top. Like shoots rising from a scorched landscape, Lyric's blonde roots showed along the part in her blue hair. Lyric and Cameryn—they had been best, if unlikely, friends, since grade school.

"Blame your mammaw—she told me to go right on up," Lyric said. "I guess you were so busy staring at yourself that you didn't hear me thumping up the steps. Of course, if I looked like you, I'd be checking me out, too." Lifting a chubby hand to her forehead, Lyric said, theatrically, "Oh, how I hate mirrors!"

"Shut up. You know you're a goddess."

"A *big* goddess."

"Not that big."

"Thank you for that, thin one. If folks would just examine their history, they'd see that larger girls like *moi* used to be the standard for beauty. It wasn't until the flapper era that skinny chicks like you pushed us out. You've ruined the curve, Cameryn. You and your legion of anorexic cousins."

It was true that Lyric took up space, but contrary to what she thought, it wasn't so much her shape as her personality. A gifted student, an artist, a mystic, Lyric was in many ways Cameryn's opposite, the fire to her ice, the yin to her yang. Outsiders would never have put the two of them together if they'd seen them on the street. With her blue hair and wild clothes, Lyric had a super-sized personality. She towered over Cameryn in height and in attitude. A crystal chanter, a New Ager, a spiritualist, Lyric often turned up her nose at Cameryn's beloved science, fought against Cammie's Catholicism, talked right over her when they were together, and made Cameryn laugh like no one else. The bond they'd formed on the playground had never been shaken. They were split-aparts—chosen sisters in the truest sense.

Lyric jumped onto Cameryn's bed and dropped the laundry basket on the floor with a resounding thud. Unlike Cameryn, Lyric wasn't known for being fussy.

"So! You weren't at work today. I came by, and they said they sent you home early. Playing hooky, huh?" Lyric accused.

"Nothing like that. Justin came by and convinced me I had to go with him to check out a body. Turned out it was a dead dog." Twirling her finger in the air, Cameryn said, "Big whoop. Or maybe—big *woof.*"

Lyric grinned. "That man will use any excuse to be with you. You realize he's in love with you."

"You are, as always, delusional."

"Deny it if you must, but you know I'm right," Lyric claimed. "I also detect a hint of reciprocation. Are my psychic powers still cranked?"

"They are nonexistent. And since you're being such a pain, I must ask the requisite question. Why are you here?"

"Because," Lyric answered, suddenly serious, "I have a message from your mother."

Cameryn felt a chill spread through her, seeping from her heart to her extremities. Hardly daring to breathe, she asked, "When did she call?"

"Today. Just now, actually. The call came into the Grand. Adam was there and he took it, but he couldn't get ahold of you. He tried—"

"I turned off my cell."

"So here I am, delivering the message."

Saying nothing, Cameryn walked to the window and looked out.

"Cammie," Lyric spoke low, "are you sure you don't want to tell your dad what's going on? I feel like we're spies or something."

"I told you, my dad checks my cell records. He checks our caller ID. If Hannah called here, he'd know."

"Tell me again why that would be such a bad thing."

"It just would, that's all," Cameryn insisted. "What did Hannah say?" Still staring out the dormer window, she watched the orange-gold sun paint the tips of the mountains as she waited to hear the newest message. She had meant to let Hannah go, just like her father and grandmother wanted . . . until that day at the Grand when the first phone call came while she was working her night shift. That was the night her mother arose once more, the night when the real secrets had started.

"Hey, kid, what are you doing staring out the window?" her father asked from the doorway. "I thought you were supposed to be folding laundry."

Startled, Cameryn snapped to attention. "Dad!" she said. "Um . . . hi."

"And hello to you, Lyric," Patrick added. "Long time no see."

Lyric's eyes had gone wide with panic. "Hello, Mr. Mahoney," she answered. "I didn't realize you were here."

"Yes, I'm very sneaky. What on earth were you two talking about? Cameryn's lost every ounce of blood from her face."

"Boys," Lyric said brightly. "We were talking about boys." Cameryn had to hand it to her: Lyric could think fast.

"Ah, that explains it. We're strange creatures, we who are the home of the Y chromosome." Leaning against the doorframe, wearing jeans and a black cable-knit turtleneck, Patrick Mahoney smiled at the girls. Then he straightened, pulling his shoulder from the doorframe. "I don't mean to rush you, Lyric, but I need to talk to the kid alone. Do you mind?"

"Not at all, Mr. Mahoney. I'm actually running off to meet Adam." Lyric's pale eyes shifted to Cameryn, silently apologizing, and then she gathered herself and hopped onto the floor. "I'll talk to you later, Cammie. Don't forget to fold the rest of your laundry."

"I won't," said Cameryn. "See ya."

"Yeah. Later. Good-bye, Mr. Mahoney." Lyric's blue hair disappeared down the hallway, like a wave retreating from the shore.

"So, Cammie, do you have a minute?" her father asked.

"I guess." Since there was only one chair in the room, she sat on her bed and pulled up her legs, yoga-style. But her father surprised her. Instead of the chair, he gestured at her bed. "Mind if I sit by you?"

Without a word, she planted her hands on her bed and raised her body so that she could scoot back into her pillows. Her father sank onto the edge of the mattress, and when he did, she noticed he looked different somehow. It took her a moment to register: Patrick, who had never been a man who would "slick himself up," as he called it, now looked as though he'd been polished. Gone was the old, thick brown leather belt, cracked and scored like elephant skin. Gone, too, were his old work boots. Today he wore new hiking boots made of fawn-colored suede and a smooth leather belt with a silver buckle. His hair seemed strangely controlled, and it took a minute before Cameryn detected the difference. His neck, which usually bristled with straggly white hairs, had been recently shaved. She thought she smelled the barest whiff of hair gel.

"How come you're so fancied up?" she asked.

"I had a meeting in Ouray."

"With who?"

"A judge."

"What judge?"

"I—it doesn't matter," he said, waving her off. "That's not what I wanted to talk to you about, Cammie. Couple of things. First, I wanted to talk to you about your job."

"My job at the Grand?" She knew she was being cagey, but she didn't like the look of intensity in her father's eyes. Just the night before, she'd overheard Mammaw's exasperated voice from behind the bedroom wall: "Patrick, your daughter needs you now more than ever. Stop putting this off—talk to the girl already!"

"What's wrong with my job at the Grand?" she asked.

"No, no, no, I'm not talking about your job as a waitress—"

"Server," she corrected.

"Server, right. What I *mean* is"—he took a breath—"your job as assistant to the coroner. Your job working for me. Mammaw tells me Justin dragged you off to look at some carcass. Did that upset you?" He hesitated, then plunged ahead. "Because I'm wondering if looking at bodies is the reason you seem . . . off . . . lately."

At this point it seemed best to stay quiet. So she just stared at him.

"Okay, 'off' may not be the right word. 'Stressed' might be better. But the point is that I can tell something's wrong. It's like you're . . . pulling away." He looked at her, his eyes anxious. "Is it all the death?"

"I still want to be a forensic pathologist," she insisted, a little too loudly. She tried again in a quieter voice. "Being assistant to the coroner is going to help me get into medical school. It'll give me an edge. You know I'm good—"

"You're about the best I've seen," he agreed, "which is pretty amazing since you're only seventeen. But your mammaw's worried that forensics is to blame for your moodiness."

"Mammaw's wrong," she answered. "If I'm moody it's my age. Teenagers are by definition grumpy. It's written on our DNA."

Nodding tersely, he said, "All right then. So we'll leave our forensic life as it is." He picked up an old stuffed animal she kept on her bed, the puppy dog she'd named Rags, then absently set it back down. "Now, for the other matter. I want to talk to you . . . about Hannah."

Cameryn felt the panic rise. Had he heard the conversation with Lyric? Did he know about the telephone call? But a quick check of his eyes told her he didn't know a thing.

She fought to keep her own expression under control. Emotions existed beneath her surface, gliding unseen through her own dark inner waters. But if her father looked at her face closely, he might be able to see what moved beneath. She knew she couldn't risk it. Everything concerning Hannah had to remain hidden—she'd promised her mother that much. Swallowing, Cameryn tried to make her face smooth. "I just had this same conversation with Mammaw," she told him. "I don't want to have it again."

"I know. It's a subject I'd rather forget about myself," he replied. "But that may have been a mistake." His hand floated to the top of her head, and she felt it press down, gently, tenderly. "You're so much like her, you know," he said. "I don't know how she looks now, but back then, your mother wore her hair long. Long and dark and curly. She was small like you, too. I didn't know how she could carry twins in that tiny body."

"Dad—*stop*. I don't want to talk about this." Cameryn pulled away from his touch, something she had never done before. He stared at her, his mouth agape for seconds or a minute, Cameryn wasn't sure which.

"Cammie," he asked, "what is going on?" He started to say something more, but the telephone rang, and a moment later Mammaw called shrilly, "Patrick! It's for you."

Her father didn't move.

Cameryn said, "Go ahead and take it."

"No. No, we need to finish this." Turning toward the door he called out, "Tell whoever it is I'll call them back, Ma." Although his head turned slightly, he kept his eyes locked onto Cameryn's as he spoke, and Cameryn returned his gaze.

Her grandmother's voice shot up again. "It's the sheriff. He says it's urgent."

"Oh, for Pete's sake. Hold on, Cammie, this should just take a minute." Reaching past her for her bedside phone, he punched the TALK button and barked, "What is it, John?"

Patrick's brows knit together as he twisted away from Cameryn. "When? . . . Are you sure?" A beat later he added, "Of course. . . . Yes, right away. We'll be right over," then tossed the phone onto the bed. He blinked hard and ran a hand through his hair, destroying its sheen.

"Dad—what happened?"

"You know Brad Oakes?" His voice was tight. It seemed he had to push from his diaphragm to get the words out.

"Yeah, I had him last year for Advanced English. Why?"

"Some kid just found him."

"Found him?" She echoed the words, buying time to stall the next words she already knew were coming.

"Sheriff says it's the strangest thing he's ever seen, and I need to get right over to make sense of it. He's dead, Cammie. Brad Oakes is dead."

Chapter Three

"MR. OAKES WAS the greatest teacher," Cameryn told her father. "He really was amazing. I can't believe he's dead."

Patrick nodded as he rolled the gurney toward the back of the family station wagon. Perched on the gurney was his "death bag," a black gear bag with the word STREETPRO stamped on the side. In it were all the tools he needed to process a scene: latex gloves, a gunshot-residue kit, paper and plastic bags, shoe covers, medical tape. Next to the death bag was a new body bag, still in its plastic, set on top of a clean white sheet that her mammaw had washed and folded. Although most body bags were not reused, the sheets always were. Mammaw bleached and cleaned them after every death and stacked them in the garage on the shelf.

"I'll wash them for you, son, but I don't want those sheets in my house," she'd declared. "They give me the willies. And don't tell me any details about what happened to the poor souls. Remember, Pat, I don't want to know."

That was another big difference between her mammaw and herself. Cameryn always wanted to know. Her father said those who worked with the dead were the last ones to hear them speak because their remains told the story, however softly spoken. If Patrick didn't hear their final whispers, no one would.

"Brad Oakes was a fairly young man," he told Cameryn now, "which makes it an even greater tragedy."

"Was it a heart attack?"

"Here, smooth the tarp down. No, I don't think it was his heart—Jacobs was going on and on about the bizarre condition of the body, whatever that means. I'm confident we'll be taking a trip to Durango for an autopsy. You got the tarp all the way in the corner?"

"Got it," Cameryn grunted, smoothing the heavy plastic—the one to protect against body-fluid leakage—into the edges of their station wagon. Since Silverton was so small and its budget so tight, the old Mahoney family station wagon had been pressed into duty, at times doubling as the county hearse. When her father was called on a case, he'd slap a long rectangular magnet, which sported the words SAN JUAN COUNTY CORONER in thick red letters, onto the driver's-side door. Once, though, her father had forgotten to put the sign on their car. She had been riding with him when they'd stopped on Greene Street, where they were approached by a tourist wanting directions. Her father had blandly explained how to get to the store named Fetch's, and the woman thanked him and walked away, oblivious to the corpse zippered into a body bag in the station wagon's bay.

Cameryn loaded the satchel, sheet, and body bag into the back of their car while her father collapsed the gurney. In sync, she helped her father slide it inside and slam the hatch shut. Then, putting his arm around her, he pulled her close and kissed her roughly on the top of the head.

"You're sure you're ready for this?" he asked. "Since he was your teacher and all?"

"I'm just glad I can help."

"It's all we can do for him now."

It was strange, Cameryn thought, the way life could change so suddenly. Ten minutes ago all she could think about was the tragedy of her mother, and here was another, more immediate heartbreak that had plunged her feelings further into the depths. *Get professional,* she told herself. *Someone has died. Do the work.*

Her analytical mind resurfaced, ready to interpret the scene and sift for clues. Patrick, too, seemed to have shoved their prior conversation into his own personal underground. Though they were father and daughter, they were now coroner and assistant to the coroner, and, most importantly, a forensic team.

Cameryn had barely slammed the door before her father backed the car out of their driveway and headed for River Street and the tiny blue home where Mr. Oakes lived. *Had* lived. Patrick's eyebrows, thick as awnings, came together as his fingers tapped the steering wheel. He was nervous, that much was clear. Whatever Sheriff Jacobs said had rattled him, which surprised Cameryn since her father didn't rattle easily.

Bizarre condition? What did that mean, exactly? Cameryn wondered. *What were they walking into?* Mostly Patrick Mahoney dealt with the garden variety passings, when ancient Silverton residents expired in sad but not unexpected ways. Those required nothing more than signing a release that allowed the departed to be taken away to a mortuary. But a questionable death like this meant pressure. From this point on, Cameryn knew, everything she and her father did would count. The coroner couldn't make a mistake because every move would be scrutinized by judges and lawyers. In the game of death, you played for keeps.

She pressed her forehead against the window and felt the chill of the glass, wishing it could cool her mind and the thoughts that seemed to fever her. The station wagon passed brightly painted, jellybean-colored houses as they headed east to Silverton's foothills. Most of the trees out here were evergreen, although every once in a while they'd pass clumps of aspen stripped bare by the cold November wind. She remembered Mr. Oakes reading a poem about seasons and how in nature things seem to die, only to be reborn in the spring. But Mr. Oakes wouldn't be reborn. He'd be buried and stay in the ground or maybe blow away in ashes. There would be no spring for him, ever again.

"Where did they find him?" she asked softly. Her breath frosted the glass.

"It seems he was found in his own bed."

"At least that sounds peaceful."

"I'm not sure about that—not from the way Jacobs was babbling about the body's condition. I guess we'll know more when we get there."

Cameryn thought about the death, but forced herself to think about his life. "Mr. Oakes wasn't married, was he?"

Her father squinted, thinking. "If memory serves he is—*was*—a single guy."

"So who was it that found him? A girlfriend?"

He shook his head. "No. Sad to say he was discovered by a Boy Scout."

It took a beat for Cameryn to register this. "A *Boy Scout* found the body? Exactly how did *that* happen?"

Her father put on his blinker and turned onto Snowden, a winding dirt road that took them close to the cemetery. "Oakes was a Scout leader—did you know that?"

"No. He was a real health-nut type of guy—a hiker and mountain biker—but I didn't know about the Scouting. Then again, I haven't been in a troop since Brownies."

"Sheriff Jacobs told me Oakes was supposed to take a group on some wilderness hike. When he didn't show, one of the Scouts went looking for him, pounded on the front door, and then let himself in. That's when he found the body. The kid's apparently pretty shook up."

Cameryn rubbed her knees through her jeans as she thought about this. "Do you know the kid's name?"

"All I know is Jacobs said he's some Eagle Scout—"

"An Eagle Scout?" She straightened and looked at her father in surprise. "Then it's got to be Kyle O'Neil. He's the only guy in Silverton who's made it that far."

"It's probably him, then. And here we are." Easing the station wagon into Mr. Oakes's driveway, Patrick turned off the ignition. But he didn't move. Instead, he rested his elbow on the steering wheel, tapping his forehead with his index finger. She could tell he wanted to say something, so she waited, outwardly patient, although her mind was already focused on what she'd find inside the blue house.

The clipboard with the coroner form was on the dashboard, so she pulled it onto her lap. Checking her watch, she entered their arrival time: 1126 military time. She'd already taken out a pair of latex gloves from the death bag, so she wriggled them on and snapped the bands against her wrists, stinging her skin. Her hair had been tied back, and the peppermint oil, perfect for covering smell if need be, was secure in her pocket. Cameras weighed down the death bag. She was ready.

Patrick sighed. "Could you stop for just a second, Cammie? I want to talk to you before we go in there."

She clipped the pen into the top of the board, not meeting his gaze. "What about?"

"We left off our last—conversation—pretty suddenly and . . . you and me—we're still good, right? You'd come and talk to me if . . . if you needed to. About Hannah." He turned his head to look at her. And for the second time in as many days, Cameryn raised her own eyes and lied straight into his clear, blue, fatherly eyes.

"You know I would," she said, marveling at her own nerve.

Relief washed over his face, and for a moment she felt a pang of regret. He was her father, after all. But now was not the time to do anything but focus on the case at hand. She swallowed her emotions so that they disappeared once again.

"We'd better get going, Dad," she said. "Look—Sheriff Jacobs is pacing in front of the window."

"Right," he said. "Let me get my bag."

Cameryn stepped onto the dirt driveway. She had never been to her teacher's home, and she was surprised at the size of it. It was small, even by Silverton standards. The house was shaped like a shoebox, long and narrow, with two giant fir trees towering past its roofline, dwarfing it even more. The shingles were dark blue while the house was a lighter shade, the exact color of the Silverton sky, which Cameryn, as a kid, had named Crayola Blue. All the way around the perimeter a plastic yellow tape had been wrapped in an uneven square, looped around the fir trees and slung across a fence post in the back. It read CRIME SCENE: DO NOT CROSS. Cameryn heard a dog barking in the backyard as she ducked beneath the tape. She was nervous, ready.

"Well hello there, Cameryn," Sheriff Jacobs said, swinging open the front door and motioning her inside. She stepped into an alcove and smelled something like rain on wool. Jacobs's jacket, maybe. "Here you are. Again," he told her.

She could feel it, the waves of disapproval radiating in her direction. There was an awkward pause, so she said, "Are you declaring this a crime scene?"

"I'm just being careful, going by the book," he answered slowly. "I've never seen anything like what's in the room back there."

"What's wrong with the body?" she asked, but Jacobs brushed her question aside.

"Told your dad he might not want to bring you, with the remains being in the condition that they are."

"I can handle it, Sheriff."

"Maybe. Maybe not. You could say your father's got a lot of faith in you. Or you could also say Patrick doesn't know where the lines are."

Sheriff Jacobs had always reminded Cameryn of a rodent. He was a diminutive man, with quick, darting movements and deep-set eyes that appeared even smaller behind his wire-frame glasses. Gray hair, so thin it showed teeth marks from his comb, had been slicked back. Although he and Patrick were friends, Jacobs always made it clear that he was not comfortable with Cameryn's job as assistant to the coroner. "I'm telling you, Pat," she once heard him say, "this job's too hard for the girl," to which her father had replied, "You let me take care of my own daughter. She's smart, and what's more, I need her."

Today the sheriff had on his regular street clothes with heavy boots laced up past his ankles. The only thing that distinguished him from the other Silverton residents was the gold five-pointed star he'd pinned onto his red flannel shirt.

"Is Deputy Crowley here?" Cameryn asked. It wasn't that she cared, but she was desperate for something to say that would break the man's laser stare from her face.

"He's in the kitchen interviewing the witness. Why don't you go on back there and help him."

But I want to see the body, she thought. *And I don't want to see Justin again. And why hadn't her father come inside? How long did it take to get equipment from a car?*

She shrugged her shoulders, cramming her hands into her jeans pockets. "No, thanks. I'll wait for my dad. So has time of death been called?"

"Del Halbrook has already come and gone. He ran the strip and contacted Dr. Kearney in Durango, so we got a declared time of death at"—he looked at his notebook and flipped back a page—"eleven hundred hours."

Del Halbrook was a volunteer firefighter, and Cameryn wasn't surprised he'd already left the scene. Procedure said the emergency medical technicians had to put leads on the decedent's chest and run an electrocardiogram strip, even if they were obviously dead, then phone in the results to a doctor in order to get a declared time of death. Her father always called the EMTs "phantoms" because they vanished from the scene so quickly. "I guess they only like to treat the living," he'd say. "There's not a lot you can do for a corpse."

She heard the heavy clump of boots behind her. "Sorry, I had to take a call," her father said, holding up his cell phone. "So what'd I miss?"

"Here's what we know so far." Jacobs shuffled through the pages of his notebook and began to read. "Brad

Oakes was scheduled to take a group of Scouts on a wilderness hike at ten A.M., departing from the Congregational Church. When he didn't show, Kyle O'Neil—do you know Kyle?"

"Vaguely," said her father.

"I do, and he's a great kid. It's a real shame he had to find the body like that." Jacobs cleared his throat and continued. "So anyway, Kyle gets sent by another Scout leader to get Oakes. Kyle says he drove up here and that he didn't see anything out of place—no other person coming or going, nothing unusual." With an index finger, Jacobs pushed up his glasses, which had slipped down his thin nose. "Kyle goes inside, finds the body, and calls me real quick. I hightailed it over here. And that's about it."

Patrick nodded, rubbing his hand over his chin. Cameryn noticed there were whiskers growing where he hadn't shaved, white stubble that looked like grains of sand. "You keep hinting that there's something strange about the body," he began, but Jacobs just shook his head.

"At this point I think it's better if you just tell me what you see, without me influencing your expert opinion, Pat. And if you want my advice"—he gave Patrick a hard look—"you should get a look at the remains *by yourself.*"

Ignoring the warning, Patrick unzipped the death bag

and handed Cameryn a pair of paper booties. "Since we don't know what we're dealing with, I'd like you to put on a pair of these, too," he said, handing a pair of blue booties to the sheriff. "I realize you've already been in the room, but if it is indeed a crime scene we want to take as little as possible in and leave even less behind."

"You're the coroner," Sheriff Jacobs said. Leaning against the wall, he twisted up one foot, then the other, stretching the blue fabric over his boot. Cameryn and her father did the same.

"Here, you'll want the camera," her father said, handing Cameryn the bag. With the booties on, the three of them padded down the hall.

Somewhere in the distance she could hear muffled voices. *It must be Justin interviewing Kyle,* she decided. The floor of the hallway was made of wood polished so smooth Cameryn felt herself slip in the booties, but her father grabbed her elbow to steady her.

They passed a small room that must have been an office. She paused for a moment at the door, curious over the precise order inside. Papers had been left on the desk, but the neat stack was perpendicular to the desk's edge and the glass top had been polished so that it shimmered as though it were made of water. Spines of books lined a bookshelf, grouped according to height, like slats in a fence. A vase filled with wild blue flax, aspen daisy, and Indian blanket flower had been set next to the telephone.

"Are you coming, Cammie?" her father called.

She answered with a nod.

"He's in the back bedroom there," Sheriff Jacobs said, pointing. His eyes shifted to Cameryn's. "You don't know what's in there. You sure about bringing—?"

"I'm sure," her father snapped. "Let's just get on with it."

She was grateful for her father's confidence, but as she walked closer to the door at the end of the hallway her throat tightened until she couldn't swallow. Her father's face was grave as he placed his hand on the small of her back, as though he might need to give her a boost inside. She leaned against the hand as he propelled her forward. Was she resisting? Curiosity mixed with fear as the door creaked open, the hinges protesting, it seemed, those who dared to disturb the dead that lay within.

"All right, then. He's on the bed, just like I found him," Jacobs said. "I'll be dogged if I know what to make of this."

Cameryn took a sharp breath, then pushed through the doorway.

In the corner of the room stood an oak sleigh bed, and in the middle of the bed were the remains of Mr. Oakes. His limbs were at odd angles, like gnarled branches of trees, the legs contracted so tight his knees made steeples beneath the cotton sheet. She could see the tip of his tongue protruding. It was a strange color, a dark gray, extending beyond his lips—a shriveled turtle's head of a tongue peeking from the edge of his mouth.

But that wasn't the horror of it. When her mind finally registered the picture, she wished, in that instant, that she'd listened to Sheriff Jacobs. Because she was looking down at the face that was no longer there. A mask, like that from a horror show, replaced the face she had known.

Skin, no longer smooth like her teacher had worn in life, had now withered to the bone. Blood seeped down his teeth like painted lashes. But the worst was his eyes. The lids of his eyes had rolled back like window shades, revealing two dark holes.

The eye sockets were empty.

Chapter Four

"SO WHAT DO you make of the eyes, Pat?" Sheriff Jacobs asked.

Patrick moved forward, peered closer, and then closer still. Straightening, he said, "Truthfully? I have no idea."

Cameryn nodded in silent agreement, the only motion she made that the others could see. Inside, she was reeling. Like her father she'd moved nearer, and now what she wanted most to do was move away again, as far away as she could go.

The gel from inside Oakes's eyes had mixed with blood, fusing into a substance that had exploded from both sockets. A starburst pattern of deep red stretched from his forehead all the way to his cheeks, and where the eyes had been were sockets that seemed filled with earth. With a start she realized the small, coin-shaped piece of brown clinging to the side of her teacher's nose was in fact his iris. In that instant she fought the bile that rose from her stomach in a hot foam. She took a series of deep, short breaths and commanded herself, *Think clinically. Leave all your emotion behind and stay professional. You've got a job to do, so do it.*

"You okay, Cammie?" Sheriff Jacobs asked, and she thought there might be a hint of smugness in his voice. "You're looking mighty pale there."

"I'm fine," she answered. Because Jacobs wanted her to fail, in a strange way it braced her, shored her up. "It's just so . . . bizarre. I've never seen anything like this."

"Well, neither have I, and I've been sheriff a lot longer than you've been assistant to the coroner. You think it's some kind of weird medical condition, Pat?"

"Maybe. I don't know, I'm not a doctor." His tongue made a clicking sound between his teeth. "I've heard of proptosis—"

Sheriff Jacobs looked at him sharply. "English, please."

"Proptosis—a bulging of the eyeballs. There are a couple of conditions that can cause it, but to have an eyeball actually explode . . ." He shook his head and let out a small stream of air through his lips, continuing, "I have to say I've never heard of that. I'm at a complete loss, John. A complete loss."

"Dad," Cameryn interrupted, suddenly remembering, "this may be way off, but I saw a dog this morning—it was on the side of the road, and it didn't have any eyes, either. It looked just like this. Do you think there could be a connection?"

"Nah," Sheriff Jacobs interjected, "my deputy told me the same thing. One's got nothing to do with the other."

Already prepared for the sheriff to blow her off, Cameryn asked, "What do you think, Dad?"

Her father's eyes half-closed as he considered it. "John's right. A dead dog left outside is bait for predators and they'll chew up remains in a matter of hours, and the eyes are always the first thing to go. But there are no predators here—inside this bedroom, I mean. Look, all the windows are shut and there's no way in or out. Scavengers didn't have access to this body, unless . . ." Patrick turned to the sheriff, who was busy scratching notes on a pad. "Wait a second—Oakes's dog was found outside, right?" he asked.

"Yep." Jacobs pointed the tip of his pen toward the window. "I know that dog—he's a spaniel named Rudy. The dog's locked up out back, just like we found him."

Cameryn understood why her father was asking. From her books she knew a gruesome fact: Pets, especially dogs, sometimes chewed on their master's remains shortly after the human's death. Her father sometimes joked that pet owners should learn to die facedown. A dog could have easily done this.

Now Patrick said, "And you're sure Kyle didn't fence the dog himself after he got here?"

"Positive. Rudy's not the cause of this mess. God only knows what is."

As the two of them spoke, Cameryn leaned closer to the body once again until she was standing just inches away. Her stomach had quieted as she concentrated on the puzzle before her. She saw the remains of her teacher, but she knew she must not think of him as that person—for now, he was evidence in a possible crime scene, the shell left behind, the remains, the victim, the corpse. She couldn't allow herself to feel what that loss meant, not yet. It was important that she copy her father's impassive face and Jacobs's cool manner. If her veneer cracked, they would ask her to leave. Unzipping the death bag, she pulled out her camera and removed the lens cap.

"Good, Cammie, get lots of pictures," her father said. "I have a feeling we're going to need them."

She began at the bottom of the bed, concentrating at first on the feet, snapping one picture after the other in rapid succession as she worked her way up. A down comforter, encased in a navy duvet and leaking feathers, had been tossed to one side. Raised knees made a tent of a pale blue sheet that stopped midway up the corpse's chest. His right hand clutched a fistful of sheet in a knot so tight the fabric made pleats, accordion style, that rippled all the way to the floor. The left side of his chest still sported three white EKG pads where Del Halbrook had attached the leads. Del had been careful, she knew, to disturb the scene as little as possible. *Snap, snap, snap*—Cameryn took picture after picture of her teacher's hands, his face, his ash-blond hair, the empty sockets, recording his remains—the remains of his life, she told herself, not just his death.

Above his head, on the wall, were two black-and-white nature prints, one depicting a snowfield glittering in the sun, the other a mountain waterfall. A white porcelain vase filled with more wildflowers bloomed from his nightstand, the same flowers that she'd seen on the desk in his office. Here, once again, were the lavender petals of the aspen daisy, the orange-red Indian blanket flower, and the delicate sky-blue flax. But there was a difference: These blossoms had withered. Each flower head drooped on a flaccid stem until the heads almost touched the nightstand's surface.

That's odd, she thought. In his classroom, Mr. Oakes hadn't been one to keep any blossom past its prime. Everything there, as in his home, had been neat and shining clean, because, he'd told them, thoughts die in chaos. The only hint of dissention in Mr. Oakes's ordered universe came from his own dark blond hair, which always fell in his eyes when he read poetry. It had been the one part of him that refused to submit. Against her will, Cameryn's teacher sprang to life in her memory, breathing and laughing and once again alive in her mind's eye.

"Remember, kids," Mr. Oakes had said, propped on the edge of his desk, "it's your job to *drink in* life. The poet Richard Wilbur wrote one of my favorite lines of all time. 'I die of thirst, here at the fountainside.'" He'd paused, then wagged his finger at them, smiling a crooked half-smile. "Think of what it means to live, and never waste a moment of it."

You didn't waste it, did you, Mr. Oakes? Cameryn thought now as she snapped pictures of the flowers before moving her lens to capture the top of her teacher's head. *Because it's gone now. You were right about living, since you never know when your time will come. . . .*

"That's good, Cammie, that's good," her father told her. He'd held the clipboard in one hand and a pen in the other as he busily checked things off, but now he came over to stand beside her. Reaching down, his gloved fingers gently grasped Mr. Oakes's jaw and moved it from side to side, which caused the gel from the sockets to gleam in the light. "He's just going into rigor now. When's the last time someone saw him alive?"

"Last night at some Scout thing. Kyle said Oakes left the group at about ten thirty P.M. That means at the most he's been dead less than . . ." Jacobs's eyes searched the ceiling. "Twelve hours."

Twelve hours, Cameryn thought. *Hardly long enough*

to digest a meal. She took in the room that had now become a time capsule and wondered how it must have looked the night before. No lights were left on in the room; she knew nothing had yet been moved or changed by Sheriff Jacobs. When Mr. Oakes died, darkness must have hidden his dresser, with its display of pewter-colored candles mounted on black onyx.

She took a picture of the framed Indian arrowhead collection, which hung on the wall next to a painting of Red Mountain. All of these, she realized, were clues to her teacher's inner world, snapshots of a man she couldn't begin to know. A man who had died alone, in this room, with only the wilted flowers as a witness.

Her father cleared his throat. "All right. I'm going to bag his hands and flip him so we can see what's on the other side. But before I do, I'd like to ask your opinion, Cammie. What do you see?"

Sheriff Jacobs snorted. "Cameryn's not going to know anything about this."

"She's assistant to the coroner, and I'm asking for her thoughts," her father replied coolly. Patrick turned to Cameryn and asked, "Any theories or observations?" He looked at her with complete seriousness, as though Cameryn would have something of value to say. In Silverton she had a reputation as a reader and researcher in the forensic field, but that was only from studying books and forensic materials posted on the Internet.

This was different. This was real life, without footnotes. She noticed that one of Sheriff Jacobs's booties had come off his heel, and it puffed around the toe of his shoe like a cupcake. The sheriff crossed his arms over his chest, a move that obscured his badge.

Cameryn lowered her camera and wrapped its plastic strap around her wrist, trying to buy time. "Well, uh, let me see," she began. "I guess we've talked a lot about his eyes—"

"We won't have an answer to that until the autopsy," her father said. "Anything else?"

"I have to say I'm kind of surprised by the position of the body."

"The position. What about it?" asked Jacobs.

"I don't know—I guess the way he's got his arms and his legs all drawn up. It looks like what happens to victims when they're burned, but it's obvious from the condition of Mr. Oakes's skin that he hasn't been. Burned, I mean. See that?" She pointed to where her teacher clutched the sheet in his hand. His fingers had blanched white, except at the tips, which were a deep purple. "There's nothing that shows scorching on the bed or bedding or anything else. And check out the sheets. They're pulled into his fist, which means he died in this bed. Whatever happened, it happened here."

"Well, you sure haven't lost your powers of observation," her father said, looking pleased. He shot the sheriff a look before adding, "And you're right about the positioning of the body. He's in a classic pugilistic stance."

"How's that?" Sheriff Jacobs asked. One of his eyebrows rose from behind his glasses as he looked from Cameryn to her father.

"Pugilist—it means a fighter's pose. It's like Cammie said, when a person dies in a fire they pull their limbs up just like we see Oakes doing here."

"That's fine and dandy, except for the obvious fact that this man wasn't burned in no fire," Jacobs snapped. "So we're back to a big fat I-don't-know." The sheriff pulled on his long nose and sniffed. "We're all just chasing our tails here. So I'm thinking I was right to put up the crime-scene tape in the first place. It might not be anything, but for now, I'm gonna treat it like a possible crime's been committed, least until I know otherwise. Agreed?"

It was at that moment that Cameryn's cell phone rang, playing the theme of *The Lord of the Rings* in silvery notes. She ignored it, but her father told her to go ahead and answer since it could be Mammaw, and if it was to tell her that they'd be a while, especially since he was going to take the body straight to Durango. Retrieving the phone from her back pocket, Cameryn flipped it open as she twisted away from Jacobs's prying eyes. Near her were the withered flowers, petals dry as butterflies' wings. There was a smell here, too. Indescribable, like burnt grass or popcorn that hadn't popped. And another odor beneath that, but it was a smell she couldn't place.

"Hello?" she half-whispered.

"Cammie? It's me, Lyric."

"Lyric, this isn't a good time—"

"Are you sitting down? If you're not you should, because wait until you hear this! There's a rumor going around that Mr. Oakes is dead! *Dead!* It can't be true, but if it is, I'm going to lie down and die myself. You know he's my favorite teacher of all time—he's the whole reason I love to write poetry and my journal and . . . Where are you, anyway?"

"How did you hear about Mr. Oakes?" Cameryn whispered fiercely, stepping to the corner of the room while plugging her ear with a latexed finger. "We just got here—I'm processing the scene right now!"

"Then it's true?" Lyric wailed. "Oh my God, I don't believe it. What happened? I heard his eyes were blown right out of his face!"

Cameryn felt a sudden pressure on her shoulder. "Is that Lyric?" She whirled around, her nerves jangling, to stare straight into the sheriff's thin face.

"What I want to know is how in the Sam Hill did this get out to the teenage population? Deputy!" He marched over to the door and yelled again, louder than before, "Deputy Crowley, I'd like you to get in here. Tell Kyle to wait in the kitchen." Then, to Cameryn, he barked, "Hand me that phone."

Cameryn had barely placed it into the sheriff's hand before he whipped it to his ear. "Lyric! Sheriff Jacobs here. I'd like to know how you're already aware of Mr. Oakes's death. . . . Adam? How did he find out? . . . You call him and ask who . . . Yes, and then call me back at . . . No, on second thought, changed my mind. I'd like you both to come down to the house. It's the blue one, 1195 River Street. . . . Good . . . Yeah, bring him with you. . . . Uh-huh, just a few questions and then you're gone. Hurry now."

He snapped the phone shut and handed it back to Cameryn, his eyes glittering. "There's nothing so aggravating as living in a small town. I swear to the Lord Almighty that Silverton's got more leaks than a colander."

"I don't know what the big deal is," Cameryn protested.

"That's because you might know bodies but you don't know law. Leaks can compromise a case, and I want to know where they came from."

"You wanted to see me, Sheriff?" Justin asked. He appeared at the doorway wearing the same outfit he had worn earlier, with the exception of his badge, which hung from a cord around his neck instead of pinned to his shirt like Jacobs's. "I was just about to let Kyle go home—"

"Keep him!" The sheriff's reply was brisk. "Take Cameryn to the kitchen and wait there for Lyric and Adam. They're on their way, and they might open up more if Cameryn's there. Find out who knew what when. Maybe I can work that thread backwards and get some answers."

"No problem. Come on, Cammie," Justin said. He gave a slight bow and waved his hand, palm-up, toward the hallway. Her father was already busy placing paper bags over her teacher's hands, so she knew she had no choice but to leave. Grudgingly, she stepped into the hallway, following Justin, her feet slipping as she skated along the floor in her booties.

"Do you know Kyle?" he asked her, his voice low.

"This is Silverton, Justin," she whispered. "Everyone pretty much knows everyone, especially if they go to school together."

"So I'll take that as a yes."

"That would be a good guess."

"What do you know about him?"

Shrugging, she said, "Straight As, football, outdoorsy, hot-looking, super-smart—your basic perfect guy."

Justin stopped moving now, so suddenly she almost ran into him. Turning, he looked down at her, his eyes intense, and Cameryn, who was almost a full foot shorter, was forced to look up. From this angle she saw how square Justin's jaw was, and how his ears looked translucent in the light. She put her hands in the back pockets of her jeans and waited, but Justin watched her, silent.

"What?" she finally said.

"I've never heard you talk that way before. Using my deductive powers, I'd say you have a thing for him."

"Nobody says 'thing' anymore, Justin," she whispered. "Let's just say every girl would like to go out with Kyle, except he usually hits on girls from Ouray or Durango. We small-towners aren't quite good enough, I guess."

Justin signaled her to lean in close; suddenly his voice was low, conspiratorial. He placed his palm on the opposite wall, effectively blocking her off from the rest of the hallway, and when he spoke, his breath was warm on her cheek. "Well now, just so you know, I don't like the guy."

"Really? Why not?" Cameryn asked. "Do you think he had something to do with—?"

"No. Nothing to do with the case—at least, nothing I can put my finger on."

"Then what?"

Justin hesitated. "There's something off about Silverton's wunderkind. He answers questions . . . but he doesn't really. It's like he's programmed. You know what I mean?" He'd taken off his jacket, and Cameryn could see a sweat stain beneath his arm. Dark blue with a tiny edge of white, the salt from his sweat, a miniature wave on a shoreline.

"I'm afraid I don't," she replied.

"I've been talking to him for half an hour, and I feel like I've verbally gone in circles. I'm asking for your help. When we're in the kitchen, I want you to try to get him to open up—you know, just to get the conversational gears moving. I'll take it from there."

She waited a beat before answering. "Except I'm assistant to the coroner, not assistant to the deputy. Interviewing witnesses is not in my contract."

A smile tugged at the corners of his lips. "So how much will your help cost the fine citizens of Silverton?"

"That's the thing—I don't think they can afford me."

"Just get him to talk, Cameryn. So far I haven't been able to get inside his head. I don't know, maybe he's got a thing with authority figures."

"You said 'thing' again."

"So I did."

He was looking at her, low-lidded, in a way she knew her father wouldn't have approved, since Justin was twenty-one and Cameryn was still in high school. But her father was in the other room taping Mr. Oakes's wrists.

"Here's a thought," Justin said softly. "Since you're demanding payment, how about I buy you lunch when we're done here? We could talk about the case, see what we come up with. You help me *and* get a lunch in the bargain, thereby killing two birds with one stone. What do you say?"

Cameryn pulled her hands from her pockets. She looked back to see if anyone was watching. No one was, so with her right hand she pushed against Justin's arm, breaking free. There was no way she could complicate her life any further than it already was, because there was no more room inside her, not for anything.

"Thanks for the offer," she replied, "but you're right. I shouldn't worry about my job description when you need help. I need to be more altruistic than that."

"Altruistic? Wait—Cammie," he stammered, "what are you talking about?"

"I mean I'll try to talk to Kyle, no strings attached. Doubt it will do any good, but I'll try."

His eyes widened. "But what about lunch and killing two birds with one stone?"

"Some other time."

As she headed for the kitchen, she felt a heaviness press against the tiny shoots of feeling she had for Justin. She couldn't allow it. The best way to survive was to not feel anything at all beyond what was demanded by the reemergence of her mother. People couldn't hurt her if she turned her soul to granite. For now, at least, she wanted to be as dead inside as Mr. Oakes. *Kill two birds with one stone.* "You can be the birds," she murmured, wanting him to fly away. "I'm the stone."

Chapter Five

"WAIT—WHAT ARE you talking about?" Justin demanded, but by then Cameryn had already made her way to the kitchen, her pale blue booties muffling her footsteps as she rounded the corner.

The first thing she noticed was that this room was as clean as the rest of the house, only more so. Afternoon sun streamed from the window over the sink to reflect off the chrome, creating pinpoint stars, and the countertops, made of inlaid cobalt tile, shimmered in pools of blue. There were plants in here, too. But these weren't fresh cut, but rather pots of mums that gave off a spicy smell, like pumpkin pie mixed with cinnamon tea. Then she saw him. At the table, his hands clasped in front, his face obscured by the window's backlight, sat Kyle O'Neil. His posture, as always, was ramrod straight, and his blond hair caught the light like a halo. He was tall—over six feet—and muscular in a way other boys in her class were not. When she saw him, Cameryn took in an involuntary breath, one that she made herself exhale softly. *Don't be stupid,* she chided herself. *Act professional.*

Because the truth was, Kyle made her nervous. He always had. Not that he'd ever really noticed her, at school or anywhere else. Kyle was at the top of the school's food chain, and ever since she could remember, he'd treated Cameryn with nothing more than polite detachment. But that didn't matter now, she reminded herself. Just as she had with Justin, she hardened her feelings. Just do the job and be done.

"Hi, Kyle," she said, slipping onto a chrome chair. She crossed her legs and pulled out a small notebook and a pen from her bag. Still wearing her gloves, she clicked the end of the pen and said, "Can I talk to you for a minute?"

He looked at her and blinked. "Hey, Cameryn. What are you doing here?"

"I'm helping out. I work for my dad."

"Your dad?"

"He's the coroner. Did you know that? Right now he's back with . . . the remains. Justin told me you found him earlier today—found Mr. Oakes, I mean. I'm so sorry, Kyle. That must have been awful for you."

Kyle nodded absently. He looked out the window, the

invisible membrane apparently still in place over his eyes. Then Justin sat down in one of the chairs opposite Kyle, leaning back so far that the top of the chair touched the wall. Arms folded, chin lifted, Justin gave Cameryn a slight nod. Since he seemed impatient for her to begin, she cleared her throat and said, "Sheriff Jacobs has officially declared this house a crime scene, Kyle, so he asked me to ask you a couple of questions. It'll only take a minute. Is that okay?"

Kyle's eyes flicked over at Cameryn. "Are you saying the sheriff thinks this is foul play?"

"No, he's not sure—nobody's sure of anything at this point. Any time there's a question, it's procedure to go ahead and declare the place where a body is found as a crime scene. It's kind of a better-safe-than-sorry thing."

It took a moment before Kyle spoke again. "So what happens now?"

"When we're done in there, my dad and I will take the body down to Durango for autopsy."

"That's where you'll cut him up." A flush crept up Kyle's neck and into the fringe of his hair. For a moment Cameryn thought he might cry, but then he took a deep breath, which seemed to steady him. "You'll go in and slice and dice his body like he's a chunk of meat. I don't want that for Brad. He—he was a great man."

"There isn't a choice," she told him. "We've got to get answers."

"Isn't there a way to find answers without turning him inside out?"

"It's science, Kyle. At this point it's the best we've got."

Kyle stared at her, and for the first time the invisible membrane seemed to slide away. She noticed his eyes were brown, but pale, the color of autumn fields after harvest, with thick lashes and straight brows. Kyle was examining her, too; his gaze took in her face, ran down the drape of her hair, then dropped to where her hand disappeared into her lap before drifting up to her face again.

"You had Oakes for English," he said. "Last year. You were in my class."

"Right. You sat way in the back and I was in front."

Justin's chair, which he'd been leaning back on, came down with a sudden bang. "Okay, can we get on with it?" he asked. There was an edge to his voice that surprised Cameryn. She'd almost forgotten Justin was in the room.

Cautiously, Kyle asked, "Get on with what?"

"I'll be straight with you," Justin replied. "The sheriff thinks maybe you'll open up more if Cammie here is asking the questions instead of me. Like how a couple of your classmates have already heard about Oakes's death. Would you happen to know how the story got out?"

"I thought Cameryn was the one who was supposed to do the asking."

Justin swept his arm toward Cameryn, palm-up. "Of course. Be my guest."

Flipping open the notebook, Cameryn clicked her pen. "Um . . . Justin already told you that the sheriff's most concerned about who knew what when. Did you call anyone about what you found here?"

"Just the other scoutmaster, Dwayne Reynolds. I phoned him right after I called 911."

Cameryn wrote down Dwayne Reynolds's name. She knew the man. He owned an old-fashioned Western photography studio, the kind where customers dressed up in turn-of-the-century gear and had their pictures printed in sepia tones. Dwayne himself sported an impressive handlebar mustache that reached all the way past his chin, and he wore a turn-of-the-century derby hat, even indoors.

"Then what happened?" she asked.

"After that I waited here, in the kitchen, exactly like dispatch told me to," Kyle went on, speaking only to Cameryn now. "The fireman came, then the sheriff, then you guys. That's it." He took a breath. "Can I go now? There's a bunch of Scouts at the Congregational Church who are losing it right now. I need to be there for them."

"Not so fast," Justin objected. "I've asked you this once, but I need to be sure: You're positive the door was locked when you arrived?"

"Yeah. Like I said, I tried it."

"And I checked out the back door and windows, and everything's sealed tight as a drum," Justin said, mostly to himself.

Puzzled, Cameryn frowned as she asked Kyle, "If the door was locked, then how did you get in?"

Kyle held up a silver key, turning it between his fingers. "Dwayne pulled it off his key ring and gave it to me when Brad didn't show."

"Why did Dwayne have Mr. Oakes's key?" Cameryn asked.

Kyle shrugged. "They're really good friends, I guess. Anyway, there was no way he could leave all those Scouts, so he sent me instead. He told me to throw water on Brad if I had to, just get him up. I drove over, knocked, rang the bell, took out the key, and then . . ." Kyle's voice drifted off. Cameryn knew what happened next. Kyle had walked into the bedroom and found his scoutmaster lying in bed with his eyes missing. It must have been like a scene in a horror movie.

"Wait a second, I'll take that," Justin said, holding out his hand for the key. Shrugging, Kyle dropped it into his palm and Justin slipped it into a small envelope, announcing, "This may or may not be a crime scene, but we've got to start treating it like one. People can't just come and go anymore, not until we've processed it."

As if on cue the doorbell chimed. Turning toward the doorway, Justin dropped his head back and groaned. "That'll be Lyric and company—they must have gone right under the DO NOT CROSS tape. I was just thinking the doorbell needs to be dusted for prints, and they go and ring it."

"She didn't know. Sheriff Jacobs told her to come right over," Cameryn protested.

"You're right, it's my fault. I should have been watching for them." Justin stood and pointed to Kyle. "Stay right there," he commanded. "We're not done yet."

Kyle's eyes narrowed as they observed Justin's retreating figure. Then he leaned toward Cameryn, his weight resting on his elbows. His features were angular, his jaw square and his nose sharp. An Adam's apple protruded from his neck. "The deputy doesn't seem to like me," he said.

Shrugging, Cameryn said, "Justin's okay. You've just got to get to know him."

"He's new in town, right?"

"Uh-huh. He's from New York. He's only been in town a few months."

"New York? Well, that explains it." Kyle sighed and ran his fingers across his scalp, disturbing his manicured hair. "Look, no offense, but I really want to get out of here. This hasn't been one of my better days, and the deputy's not improving my mood."

"I don't think it will be much longer."

"It's just—it feels like *I'm* the one getting grilled." Kyle pushed back his chair and stood. He walked over to the sink and was about to get some water when Cameryn warned him not to touch anything. A black, long-sleeved T-shirt, snug around his shoulders but loose at his waist, hung past his narrow hips. On his feet he wore running shoes that appeared expensive, yet his jeans were worn. An army-green parka had been slung over the back of a chair. Cameryn hadn't noticed it while he was sitting.

She could hear Justin's voice rumble in the background and Lyric's booming in reply. Adam's quieter tones wound in between, like notes from an instrument. She felt awkward, sitting there, so she said, "Do you know Lyric?"

"I haven't really talked to her. I know who she is, though. And Adam's that strange kid, the one always dressed in black."

"They're both really great," Cameryn said, feeling the need to defend them just as Kyle surprised her by saying they seemed like cool kids.

"You, too, actually," he added. He came back to the table and slid into his seat, facing her, closer than he'd been before. She noticed his hair shimmered, like golden metal shavings, and his eyes, too, had flecks of gold. "You know, I'm sorry I've never connected with you too much before this. You're easy to talk to."

Cameryn swallowed, her mouth suddenly dry. "Thanks. You, too," she mumbled.

"And I was just thinking that in a way, you're the only one who can really understand what's happened here. I could tell my friends, but they'd never be able to even imagine what we saw in that room." He leaned back into the chair and shook his head. "I mean, man, this whole thing has been so freaking weird! It's mind-blowing. You're in the business—have you ever seen anything like it?"

"Never."

"But you've seen some really bad stuff, right?" His eyes searched hers, and she looked at the table top, tracing her finger along the edge. She drew a plus sign, then a minus, her fingertip barely grazing the surface.

"Yeah, I have," she admitted. "I've seen accidents and a murder victim and . . . it's hard. Harder than I thought it would be."

"So how do you deal with it? With the gross stuff and the death and all the pain? How do you do it?"

"That's the thing, Kyle. Sometimes I don't. Sometimes, *not* dealing is the only way. It's like I just . . . separate. Like I become this other person. It's as if I'm watching myself and somehow I'm not the one zipping the corpse into the bag, but it's just my hands doing it. I mean, it's me, but it's not." She flushed, because she suddenly heard how stupid she sounded, but when she raised her eyes, he was nodding, thinking.

"I think I know exactly what you mean."

"You do?"

He nodded again. It seemed as though he was about to say more, but suddenly, Justin appeared in the kitchen. This time the deputy crooked his finger at Cameryn, announcing, "I found the leak—it was Dwayne Reynolds. I guess once he heard the news the story spread like wildfire. It just shows you how fast gossip travels in a small town. Anyway, Lyric and Adam want to talk to you before they go. I told her you were working, but Lyric, dramatic as ever, says it's *really* important. They're waiting for you outside." He glanced from Cameryn to Kyle, then back to Cameryn, frowning, his eyebrows creasing together, his lips pressed hard. "So, Cameryn, I guess you're done in here."

"Okay, then." She shut the notebook, useless since it had only two words written inside, and said, "Good luck, Kyle. I'll see you around."

"Yeah." Kyle gave her a halfhearted wave. "See ya."

At that moment the sheriff's voice thundered down the hallway, like a sonic boom. "Deputy Crowley—could you come back here? Now!"

"I'll be right there, sir!" Justin called back. For the

briefest moment, Justin stared at Kyle. Then he said, "Stay here, Kyle. Cameryn, you need to hurry. Your dad is waiting."

"All right, all right, I'm going," she said to Justin's disappearing back. She stood, but before she could leave, Kyle touched her hand.

"Wait," he said, his voice tentative. "I was wondering . . ." He straightened himself, his eyes locking onto hers. White commas indented the edge of his mouth, and with a start Cameryn realized he actually looked nervous. "I was thinking that later, maybe—would it be all right if I called you? I mean, so we could talk. About Mr. Oakes and what happened."

Cameryn considered the possibility. Kyle O'Neil. Calling *her*. Last year the thought would have been elating. But as quickly as she entertained the thought, she dismissed it. She was barely keeping her inner life together as it was—one more thing added to the emotional levee, and everything would spill over. Now was not the time to hang with Kyle O'Neil any more than with Justin. What she'd decided before had been right. Sometimes it was better not to feel at all.

She pulled her hand away, but it was as if his fingertip left a trace of energy, as if it had left its own electrical current on her skin. "You know, I'm actually not the best company right now," she answered slowly. "There's a lot going on in my life, apart from Mr. Oakes and all of this.

Actually, I'm kind of on overload. I wouldn't be much help."

He managed a half-smile. "I'm good with overload. Maybe what's supposed to happen here is that we talk. Maybe I'm the one who's supposed to help you."

She shook her head, saying, "I don't think so."

"You're sure?"

"It's just a timing thing. I'm sorry, Kyle."

Although he looked disappointed, he answered, "Not a big deal. If you change your mind, give me a call. I'm the only O'Neil in town."

"I will. And Kyle, don't let Justin get to you. The way the body looked has got everyone rattled."

"I know it. This whole thing has definitely been surreal."

"Definitely," she echoed.

She tried to untangle her thoughts as she left the house, but Cameryn had barely stepped outside into the pale November sun when she heard Lyric call out her name with such anguish it drove everything else from her mind.

"Cammie—I can't even believe our teacher's dead!" she cried. "I just talked to him last week and—what *happened* in there?"

Hovering beyond the tape, no doubt exactly where Justin had ordered her to stay, stood Lyric, her plump cheeks red with emotion. Next to her slouched Adam.

He'd already lit a cigarette, a habit that both Cameryn and Lyric had tried to discourage. Inhaling deeply, Adam took the cigarette from his mouth and flicked his ash into some rocks lining the driveway. His black hair, dyed and parted in the middle, made him appear paler than he already was.

"Hey, Cameryn," Adam said. "How goes it?"

"Well, to be honest, I've been better."

"So you're back on ghoul patrol. Is it true that Oakes sort of . . . exploded?"

"Don't be insensitive," Lyric chided. "You didn't have Mr. Oakes, but I did and so did Cameryn. You know ever since I found out I've been crying my eyes out."

"'Crying your eyes out' is a poor choice of words," Adam replied blandly. "Under the circumstances."

"Shut *up!*" Lyric demanded. "This isn't funny."

"Okay, okay!" He held up his hands, his fingernails tipped in black, saying, "I was just trying to lighten the mood. Sorry if it was too much. Hey, come here," he said. "It's going to be okay." Adam pulled Lyric close while she went limp against his shoulder. They were an odd pair, Cameryn thought—Lyric, with her ample frame, next to Adam, who was thin and sunken-chested, pale as milk. And yet they'd found each other, which meant that now Cameryn had to learn how to share her best friend. Ducking beneath the tape, she reached out and hugged Lyric until Adam stepped away.

"What happened to Mr. Oakes?" Lyric wailed. "How did he die?"

"We're not sure. No one really knows anything yet. I was just interviewing Kyle O'Neil—"

"Kyle?" Lyric blinked back tears. "What's he doing here?"

"Kyle's the one who found Mr. Oakes. Look, I know you want answers, but at this point we haven't got a clue what went on in that house. I promise, though, we'll find out."

"It's all so horrible. I mean with the eyes—"

"I know," she agreed. "But Lyric, I've got to get back inside. I'm actually getting paid, and I've got work to do, and I don't want anyone to get upset with me. Are you okay now?"

"Yeah, I'm okay." Lyric snuffled loudly while Adam dropped his cigarette and crushed it beneath his heel. He was giving Lyric a strange look.

"Come on, Lyric," he said. "Why don't you tell her so Cammie can get back to work and we can go home?"

"That's right," Cameryn said. "Justin told me you had a message for me. What's up?"

Lyric hesitated. She rubbed the palm of her hand across the apple of her cheek and blinked hard. It didn't look as though she'd washed her hair that morning, so it lay flat against her skull, which made it appear as if blue fingers clutched her head.

"I don't know if now is the time," she began. "With all the other stuff going on." She shot Adam a worried glance, then began. "I went back to the Grand to hang out with Adam while he was bussing tables, and then the phone rang. Adam gave the phone to me . . ." Her voice drifted off.

Cameryn urged her, "Just tell me. They need me inside."

At that moment her father appeared at the door, instructing Cameryn to bring in the gurney. Lyric waited patiently until Patrick was safely inside before speaking. "It was your mom again."

Cameryn froze. "Hannah?"

Lyric nodded. "She thought you might be back. You're supposed to be working. So she gave me the message instead."

"What did she say?" Cameryn asked. She could feel her eyes going wide and scared.

"Hannah said to tell you . . ." Lyric hesitated.

With a quick backward glance, Cameryn put her arm around her friend and leaned her ear close to Lyric's mouth. "*Tell* me," she said softly. Cameryn's entire head had begun to hum, as though a tuning fork had been placed beside her bones. Or maybe it was just the sound of her pulse.

"She bought a car, Cam. She's left New York."

Another twang of the fork. Cameryn's thoughts began to vibrate, louder.

"Hannah called it a pilgrimage. She said it might take a few days if she drove fast—a week at the most."

"I—I don't understand," she stammered.

"Cammie, Hannah's coming here. To meet you. She's coming to Silverton. And she's already on her way."

Chapter Six

"SO I THINK the plan is for Sheriff Jacobs to marry Justin Crowley," her father told her. "They've asked me to be the bridesmaid. I said I would do it."

"Uh-huh," Cameryn replied absently. She was staring out the window as they drove through downtown Durango, their station wagon making slow, steady progress through narrow streets jammed with cars. Banners sporting cornucopias and turkeys hung along Main Street, proclaiming the approach of the Thanksgiving holiday, while retail stores hopscotched past Thanksgiving directly to Christmas. On either side of the street, motorized Santas waved, reindeer nodded illuminated heads, lights festooned every shop window so that they glowed like a mini Las Vegas, and yet Cameryn registered none of it. Not even the body of her teacher, gently rocking in the back with every jolt of the car, could pull her from her thoughts. Hannah was coming to Silverton, and Cameryn's mind could only repeat that fact, again and again.

"Did you know we Mahoneys come from a line of leprechauns that goes all the way back to the Druids?" Patrick asked. They were stopped at a light, and his hand gently touched her shoulder, startling her. Blinking, Cameryn stared at her father.

"I'm sorry," she said. "What did you say?"

"I've been giving you a bit of the blarney, not that you'd notice. Where's your head?" When he turned to look at her, his black knit turtleneck caught the hairs on the back of his neck.

"I'm just thinking."

"About your teacher, Mr. Oakes." Her father didn't frame this as a question, so Cameryn nodded in agreement.

"About the autopsy," he added.

She nodded again.

Patrick's pale blue eyes became anxious, flicked toward her, then darted to the body bag in the station wagon's bay before returning to her face. She could see him trying to work things out. As his fingers drummed the steering wheel, he mentally put the pieces together, adding up the numbers and getting the sum wrong. He thought she was upset by the body stiffening up behind her, thought she was grieving over her teacher. *Well, let him put two and two together and get five*, she decided. *I don't need questions right now.*

"Listen to me, Cammie: There's no shame in backing out of an autopsy. I've told you before, if you're going to be able to handle the slice-and-dice, you've got to detach."

Funny, Cameryn thought. *That's exactly what I'm doing.* Another click inside, and she separated herself again, as though she were a mirror that could be split into smaller and smaller pieces, each bit able to refract an ever-shrinking image. A part of her worried that she might become too fractured to ever be whole again, that her emotions were shards that would have to be reassembled later.

"It's out of the ordinary for Moore to do the autopsy on a Saturday," her father was saying, shifting gears. "When I called him he said, 'Fascinating case, Patrick. Bring the remains down and I'll get right on it.' It's amazing he's agreed to work on his day off, but I guess the MEs do that sometimes."

"Bet he'll bill Durango double for working on Saturday," Cameryn said, relieved the conversation was going in a different direction.

"No doubt." Patrick cleared his throat and shot her a sideways glance. "Try not to antagonize him this time, okay?"

Cameryn felt her eyes go wide. "I won't! I *didn't!*"

"Ah, but you know that's not true," he countered. "If you recall, the good doctor threw you out of the last autopsy—"

"Okay, maybe I was a bit . . . aggressive . . . but I was right, wasn't I?" She remembered the detail she'd discovered, and Moore's violent reaction over Cameryn being the one to discover it. She remembered him swelling with rage and how he'd ordered her out of the room. But she also remembered that he'd helped, too, later, when it really counted. Dr. Moore was an enigma.

"All I'm saying is that sometimes life requires *diplomacy.* Moore can be an egomaniacal windbag, but he's a great medical examiner and he's going the extra mile with this case. Let's not have any trouble today."

"Whatever you say. Boss." She flashed him a smile, a compensatory tactic that she hoped would calm him. It seemed to work. His features softened, especially his eyes, ice-blue and ringed in laugh lines that sprayed from the corners.

"That's right. I'm senior management. Try not to forget it, kid."

"As long as I've got management's ear, I'd like to put in for a raise."

"Solve this case and we'll talk."

It felt good to be back in their rhythm, their father/daughter banter. Even if they both knew it was forced.

The smile on her father's face barely covered the worry that flowed beneath it, like a stream gurgling beneath the ice. The Mahoneys knew how to keep up appearances.

They had pulled into the back alley now, where the flat-roofed building squatted bleakly behind Mercy Medical Center. It was a structure so unremarkable it seemed impossible from its exterior to divine its real purpose—dissecting the dead and reading their entrails like the ancient oracles Mr. Oakes had told them about in class. The alleyway led to two metal doors, which rolled open when her father tapped his horn. Ben, the diener, waved his thickly muscled arms in the air, welcoming them inside. He wore faded green scrubs and running shoes spattered in what looked like dried blood. Cameryn noticed that he'd shaved his head so smooth his scalp gleamed, dark as chocolate.

"I was hoping Ben would be on duty today," her father said.

The diener assisted the medical examiner in the most grisly jobs, including sewing the corpse back together after autopsy when the dissection was done. Her father told her Ben was the best diener he'd ever seen, because in all the cases he'd worked on, Ben had never once lost his composure. "Even if he's plucking maggots from someone's mouth, he keeps his cool," her father once told her.

Craning over his shoulder, Patrick backed the station wagon into the garage. After the two of them hopped out, Ben unlatched the hatch and lifted it. Then, with an expert motion, he tugged the gurney as the wheels unfolded and banged onto the cement floor. The blue body bag remained perched atop it, misshapen because of the position of Mr. Oakes's arms and legs. It seemed as though they had bagged a prizefighter who was trying to punch his way out.

"Hey there, Pat," Ben said. "Cammie. Long time no see. So this vic's got no eyeballs, eh? No wonder Moore called us in—we got us a bona fide mystery here!" Then he added, "I thought you might have had enough of us the last time, girlfriend. You a glutton for punishment?"

"Mr. Oakes was my teacher."

"Your teacher, huh?" Ben's head dipped down as he began to push the gurney. "Sorry for your loss." He didn't try to say anything more, didn't parrot words to make her feel better. His "sorry," delivered in his deep baritone, was enough.

"Does Dr. Moore know I'm here?" She felt a flutter when she asked this.

"Oh, yeah, the dragon master mentioned you by name," said Ben. "The weird thing is, I think Moore has actually taken a shine to you. If the man shines on anyone besides himself, that is."

Ben and her father moved the gurney up a concrete

ramp, and with his backside Ben hit the door so that it swung open.

"What do you mean 'shine'?" Cameryn asked as she fell in step with them. She had to walk double-time to keep up. "Are you implying Moore actually *likes* me now?"

"Tolerates. In my opinion he's up to simple toleration. He respects what you did to help catch the Christopher Killer, but he's not convinced that wasn't a flash in the pan. And before you go getting discouraged," Ben told her, "remember this: when you're rating Moore's opinions, simple toleration's a good thing."

Patrick, his hand on the end of the gurney, helped steer the corpse down the narrow hallway. They pushed the gurney beneath the ceiling's round lights, which reminded Cameryn of the ones in an operating room, the kind women gave birth under. But these had an entirely different purpose. These were birthing lights in reverse. She noticed, too, that in their glow, her skin took on a green cast.

She'd been here before, and she remembered the used, hand-me-down feel of the place. Its brown carpet was worn in the center, like thinning hair, and the walls had been painted a flat, lifeless beige. There were several small rooms on both her right and her left, their doors ajar. As she sped past them, she got just a flash of what lay inside: feeble plants expiring, some wilting on shelves, others dying in corners, and plain chairs with metal legs.

It was the smell, however, that let visitors know exactly what kind of building this was. It wasn't a strong odor, but more like a hint in the air, wafting just beneath the scent of disinfectant. The charnel smell had fused into the paint, the walls, even into the very plants themselves, as though the corpses passing through had left a whisper of themselves behind, a scent that said, *My body was here.*

"Are we taking him to X-ray first?" she asked Ben.

"Uh-huh. I'll pop him in for a quick film. The dragon master's talking with the deputy and the sheriff in the autopsy suite, so you two go on ahead. Last I saw, they were into it pretty deep, trying to figure out what in the world could cause eyes to blow."

"Justin's already here?" Cameryn asked, surprised that he'd made it ahead of them.

"So it's *Justin* now, is it?" Ben's dark eyes twinkled. "Last time you were here it was 'Deputy.' Um-mm-mm. First time I saw the two of you together I thought I sensed something. Today Justin barely cleared the door when he asked, 'Is Cameryn here?' He looked mighty disappointed when I told him you weren't. What has been goin' on in Silverton, is what I want to know."

Her father stiffened. His white hair, still under the gel's control, seemed to bristle with indignation as he growled, "My daughter is only seventeen. The man's a *deputy*."

Ben smiled tolerantly. "Sorry. I was just making conversation."

It seemed best to keep quiet, so Cameryn gave the gurney a hard push, as if she and Mr. Oakes alone were streaking for the finish line.

"Slow down, Cammie," her father called after her. "This isn't a race!"

She pretended not to hear, stopping so suddenly outside the X-ray room that Mr. Oakes's body shifted forward; she had to place her hand on what she guessed was his knee to steady him.

Opening the door to X-ray, she saw that the place was no bigger than a walk-in closet. A large white machine with a movable arm stood at the ready. Behind it, a revolving door led to the darkroom, painted black. Ben stepped neatly around her, his white shoes, mottled with red, squeaking on the tile. He pulled a heavy apron from a hook and shrugged it on, telling them to leave the room, please, because of radiation. "You two go on into the autopsy suite," he instructed. "I'll bring the decedent down in two minutes. You remember the way—first door on the right past the drinking fountain. You can't miss it."

Back outside Cameryn heard a woman's laughter echoing down the hallway, ending in an abrupt, "No *way!*" followed by a disembodied, "Are you *serious*?" Life went on, even in the morgue.

"Cammie, wait," her father said, hurrying beside her. He was panting a little, and his face looked flushed. "I hope you aren't upset with me."

"About what?"

"The crack I made about Justin. About you being too young for him and him being too old for you—which he is, by the way."

"Forget it."

He fell in step beside her. "After I said it, well, I started thinking. Your mother was much younger than I was when we met—did you know that?"

"No."

"So I thought—when I said that about Justin, you might think I was being hypocritical."

"Actually, the only thing I'm thinking is that your timing sucks. This is a morgue, Dad, not a shrink's office. We can talk later."

"Except with you there's no 'later.' You're going away from me, Cammie. Maybe we should just take a chance and talk, no matter where we are."

She stopped then, her hand touching the glass rectangle of the autopsy door. Inside she could see Dr. Moore hunched over the sink. He wore thick rubber gloves, the kind people used to wash dishes with.

"Cammie? Is it your mother?"

She turned. Through tight lips she asked, "Why are you doing this? We've never talked about Hannah before, and now it's like you can't stop bringing her up. I'm walking into an *autopsy*, Dad. Leave it alone, okay? Leave *her* alone!"

Stricken, he said, "I'm sorry. I—a friend told me I should bring it up in natural conversation. About Hannah, I mean, and not make a big deal out of the subject."

"Your friend was wrong. I never even think of Hannah anymore. Not ever. Now let's go in there and do our jobs, okay?"

She smacked her palm on the swinging door and wondered at the indignation in her voice, at her dramatic flair and her father's sheepish response. Lying, it seemed, was easy, and it was getting easier all the time. Each falsehood greased the wheel for the next.

It wasn't always so. Mammaw had spooned the idea of mortal and venial sins into her along with her baby food, and even now she knew exactly which commandment she was breaking—number eight: *Thou shalt not bear false witness.* Her grandmother had given her a bracelet where each commandment was a tiny charm. The ten trinkets chimed together with every flick of her wrist, miniature bells reminding her not to sin. But now the bracelet was too small and her questions too great.

All this Cameryn considered, then dismissed, as she stepped through the portal.

The Durango autopsy suite was the size of three of her high-school classrooms, but with nothing inside to break the monotony of steel and tile. No plants to add color, no wood to take out the chill—just gleaming surfaces, cold and ready. Three autopsy tables, with their drain plugs to allow seepage of body fluid, were lined up by the sink. In the rear were large, side-by-side stainless-steel doors. She remembered it from her last visit; inside the walk-in refrigerator were brains floating in formaldehyde and pieces of heart and other organs, waiting in liquid formation, like vegetables in a market stand.

On the other end of the room was a cavernous sink, and next to it puttered Dr. Moore, his back toward them. Intent, he placed one tool, then another, on a cotton towel. Knives, saws, scissors with needle-sharp points, specimen jars—all had been laid out on the cloth in a perfect row, like piano keys. A yellow bucket had been tucked beneath the autopsy table, destined to hold left-over organs, while pruning shears, purchased at Home Depot, lay ready to bite through her teacher's breast-bone and ribs. Justin and Sheriff Jacobs were nowhere to be seen.

"Well, well, well, if it isn't our protégé," Dr. Moore said, turning to face her. "We meet again." His voice was cordial, but his face betrayed no emotion, and his eyes were hard as they examined her closely.

"Hello, Dr. Moore."

"So, Patrick, you brought her back into the nether-world."

"She's still my assistant," her father replied. "She's proven what she can do."

"That assessment may be premature. But I'm nothing if not a humble man, ready to change my opinion if it's warranted. I must admit I'm curious about you, Miss Mahoney. You seem to have intelligence. More than what is at first apparent."

Dr. Moore wore a plastic apron over his ample middle. He had a pugnacious face: An underbite pushed his lower jaw forward, which caused the folds of his cheeks to droop past his jawline. Beneath the thick, bullfrog neck, below the ample torso and Santa belly, two thin legs emerged, looking as though they belonged to another, more slender body.

"We've got ourselves an interesting case," Moore said. "Will you be solving this one, too, Miss Mahoney?"

"I'm here to help in any way I can," she answered.

"You realize it would be easier for me to take you seriously if you wore something besides a hoodie and jeans."

"I didn't plan to be here today."

"No matter. Get your scrubs on and then come back to the table," he ordered. "I've got a job for you."

Chastised, Cameryn went to the cabinet and opened

the metal door. Inside she found more disposable booties, these pale green; a plastic apron; a hair-covering
that looked like a paper shower cap; latex gloves; and
a paper mask shaped like a muzzle. She tied on the
apron and quickly braided her hair, shoving it inside
the cap, which for some reason made her feel foolish.
Tugging on the latex gloves and then the booties, she
left the mask inside the cabinet. No one here seemed
to use them.

Dr. Moore looked at her feet. "Your next purchase
should be morgue shoes."

"Morgue shoes?"

"Those of us in the business leave a pair of shoes here,
in the building. That way we don't drag any of the decedent back into our own pristine homes." In her direction
he swiveled a foot shod in black high-tops. If there was
blood on them, it didn't show.

"They say you've got a sixth sense, Miss Mahoney.
Do you?"

Cameryn shrugged modestly. "I don't know if I'd call
it a sixth sense. . . ."

"Never devalue yourself—if you're good, say so."

"I'm good," Cameryn told him, raising her chin.

"Perfect. So am I." He looked at her with his small,
deep-set eyes. She hoped he couldn't hear her heart,
beating inside her chest like a rabbit's.

Her father seemed subdued as he carefully suited up,

so Cameryn thought it best to leave him alone. Justin and the sheriff stepped out of the refrigerator—what they were doing in there Cameryn couldn't tell—and at that moment Ben wheeled in and parked the gurney parallel to an autopsy table.

"The decedent's been x-rayed, so we're ready," he announced. "Let the fireworks begin."

"Shall we, Miss Mahoney?" Moore asked, sweeping his arm toward the gurney.

Ben grabbed the bag, as did Patrick. "On the count of three," Ben said, and in a seamless motion the blue bag slipped onto the cart.

Intent, Cameryn watched the doctor's face as he unzipped the bag, a sound that, in the quiet of the room, seemed as loud as a dentist's drill. Gently, Ben unwrapped the white sheet enfolding Mr. Oakes. The left fist emerged, still clutching the sheet that was no longer there, then the right, his fingers bent into the shape of an eagle's talon. Oakes's knees, still drawn to his chest, gave a strange impression: Cameryn realized if the body were rocked forward, Mr. Oakes could kneel on his rigor-stiffened legs.

Moore frowned as if puzzled. "What on earth happened to this man?" He slipped on a pair of glasses, which magnified his eyes so that they were the size of silver dollars. Leaning so close Cameryn thought the tip of his nose might touch the corpse's cheek, he said,

"I half-expected you were exaggerating, but . . ." He put a gloved finger on Mr. Oakes's cheek and tugged. The bottom inner lid was a grayish brown, the color of dirty water, while the tiny, spidery veins looked like bits of black thread. "It appears the eyes actually burst in their sockets."

"I've been in this business a long time, and I've never seen anything like it," Ben agreed softly.

Cameryn and her father moved closer, and Sheriff Jacobs and Justin crowded in, too. Although they remained in their street clothes, they were as close to the body as those dressed in scrubs. Their six heads practically touched as they huddled close, like beads on an abacus.

Justin's hand drifted to his nose. "The smell's worse now. What *is* that stench?"

"His body is beginning to break down," Cameryn answered. "It's the smell of decay."

Dr. Moore shook his head. "No, Miss Mahoney, it's not. I'm not sure what it is, but I've been around bodies in every stage of putrefaction, and this smell is clearly quite different."

Cameryn blushed at her mistake, but no one seemed to pay it any mind.

Under the glow of the fluorescent lights, the sockets still gleamed, but the gel on the cheeks had dried and the cornea had withered like a dehydrated leaf. She registered her teacher's near nakedness. He wore only boxer shorts, white with blue stripes, and for some reason the intimacy of knowing the kind of underwear her former teacher wore made her uncomfortable. She had to remind herself that he wasn't really here. He was nothing more than a husk, as empty as a shell on the shore. But she couldn't help feeling his vulnerability on this cold metal table, where dignity, like clothing, was stripped away one piece at a time.

Sheriff Jacobs scratched his neck. "So what's the verdict, Doc? Do you think this is a homicide?"

"I couldn't possibly make that determination yet," Dr. Moore snapped. "The vitreous is dry," he said, turning back to the remains. "Strange. Very, very strange. Let's get some photographs. Miss Mahoney, you're up."

Cameryn snapped picture after picture while Ben took fingernail scrapings, everything done by the book. Eyebrow and head hairs were plucked and placed into tissue, then into coin envelopes, which were sealed, then signed. A twelve-inch Q-tip was slipped down Oakes's throat, the contents smeared onto a slide. Finally, they rolled the body on one side, then the other, as Ben tugged the bag and sheet free. Her father shielded her view while Dr. Moore yanked off the boxer shorts, made more difficult due to the angle of the legs.

"It's all right now," he whispered into her hair. She saw

that one of the men had draped a washcloth discreetly over her teacher's groin. And then came the crunching sound, like knuckles being cracked, and she watched in horrified fascination as Ben pushed all his weight against her teacher's stiff arms.

"What are you doing?" she cried.

"Gotta break rigor so we can cut him open," he huffed. "Man, he's tight." One by one, Ben worked on pushing the limbs down, each of which drifted back to position the minute he moved on. Finally, he said, "I think that's as good as we're gonna get him."

The autopsy knife glittered in reply as Moore said, "Let's see what's inside." His voice shifted suddenly, becoming more clinical, Cameryn suspected, for her benefit. "As you know, Miss Mahoney, we start with the classic 'Y' incision." With the razor-sharp blade he whipped the knife, starting from her teacher's right shoulder and slicing to the small bump on the end of the rib cage. Next came the left shoulder. Moore cut to the rib cage and all the way down to the pubic bone as he flayed her teacher open. A smell rose from the insides, and Cameryn, her hand cupping her nose, was sorry she'd left the mask behind. Dr. Moore stopped, astonished.

His hands trembling, Dr. Moore said hoarsely, "Look at the flesh."

Five heads craned in. Sheriff Jacobs and Justin

pinched their noses, while Patrick and Ben kept their hands at their sides.

"What is it, Doc?" Sheriff Jacobs asked.

With the tip of his knife, Dr. Moore cut back the fat from the flesh. "My God," he said. "This man was cooked alive!"

Chapter Seven

FOR A MOMENT no one moved. Cameryn looked on, dazed, at the flesh exposed over the rib cage. It was dark brown at the top of the "Y" incision, less so at the groin. Dr. Moore retracted the skin at the top of the Y and folded the flesh up and over Brad Oakes's face. The fat looked different, too: Instead of bright yellow, it had turned a sickly gray-brown.

"Look at the muscle here. Are you people sure he wasn't in a fire?" Dr. Moore demanded.

"He wasn't in any fire that we could see," Patrick replied.

Sheriff Jacobs agreed. "I was in that room, Doc, and there wasn't no fire in there. The bedding wasn't singed in any way. Neither was the mattress or the nightstand or anything around the guy."

"Besides, if he was in a fire, wouldn't the skin itself be burned?" Cameryn asked.

"Normally, if there was sufficient heat to cook flesh, the answer would be 'yes.' But this case seems anything but normal. I suppose we'll know more when we get inside the lungs to check for inhaled smoke." Dr. Moore's scalpel was poised in the air, like a conductor's baton, winking in the light. His face was grim. "Let's proceed," he said.

With one hand Dr. Moore yanked back the flesh, and with the other he sliced beneath it, pulling skin and fat away from the rib cage with strong fingers as he made his way to the groin. As he folded the rubbery flesh toward the table and onto Mr. Oakes's side, the bowels were exposed, shiny and dark. To Cameryn, it seemed as though the doctor were turning down a bed. Moore did this on the corpse's other side as well. Now the ribs were fully exposed, like the slats on a blind. Dr. Moore pressed his thumb into the ribs and pushed in a hard line.

"These aren't broken, but they feel strange to the touch. For lack of a better word, the ribs feel . . . dry." Moore's chin dipped, fattening his neck. "Miss Mahoney, you say you want to go into forensics. Run your fingers down the rib cage and tell me what you feel."

Cameryn looked at him in disbelief. Eyes wide, nerves jangling, she looked at the exposed ribs, then back to Moore's face, then back to the ribs once more.

"Just run your fingers over the breastbone, like this."
Once again Dr. Moore rubbed his thumb along the
bones, which gave way beneath his touch. His eyes
hardened as he asked, "Or are you too squeamish,
Miss Mahoney?"

Her father was standing just beyond the autopsy
table, and she could see him shake his head slowly,
almost imperceptibly. He'd put on a mask, which had
the effect of making the hairs of his eyebrows appear
more like brush. *You don't have to,* he said silently. *It's
not required.*

Cameryn looked again at the exposed remains of her
teacher. What her father didn't understand was that
she wanted to do this. To get this close to the source
of life, even life that had been extinguished, fascinated
more than repelled her. She took a quick gulp of air,
then, moving close, she reverently placed her latexed
hand against Brad Oakes's ribs and ran the tips of her
fingers lightly up and down. She felt the jut of each
bone, like knuckles on a clenched fist.

"Push harder," Dr. Moore barked. "You won't hurt
him."

Her fingers weren't as strong as the doctor's, but she
could feel the ribs give way as she pressed against the
bone.

"I don't know what I'm feeling for," she said.

"True enough. But I want you to file this sensation away

in your brain. These ribs are not normal. Step back."

Cameryn did. She realized with a start that at the end of each finger, her gloves had turned a greasy brown.

Using the pruning shears, Dr. Moore snapped through bone, breathing more heavily as he strained against the breastbone. "Slightly osteoporotic," he huffed. He removed the breast plate. Shaped like the T from a T-bone steak, the rib plate was set aside on a separate cart that held a small sink with water flowing through it. The water made a soft gurgling sound, like a garden fountain.

"I'm going in for the heart," Dr. Moore said. His hands slipped beneath the remaining ribs so that only the area from the wrist up was visible. Through this opening he pulled the heart an inch above the ribs, still attached inside. It looked almost gray against his bright yellow gloves.

"Coronary artery, posterior descending," he said, pinching the heart between his thumb and forefinger. "Anterior descending." Squeezing harder, he suddenly stopped. "Something is definitely off here. The heart feels harder than normal."

"Heart disease?" Patrick asked.

"No." Moore sliced inside, cutting the heart free.

As he raised it up, his eyes widened and Ben said, "Oh my Lord."

Alarmed, Cameryn asked, "What?" Neither one of them seemed to hear.

"Ben, give me the long knife," Dr. Moore ordered.

Immediately Ben handed Dr. Moore a long-bladed instrument. With an expert motion, Dr. Moore flayed the heart open in his hand. And now her father went white as he whispered, "Good God."

"Could one of you tell us laypeople what in the Sam Hill is so strange here?" Sheriff Jacobs demanded. Fists clenched, he rocked forward onto his toes. "What are you all worked up about?"

"The heart. Man, I've been around a lot of bizarre stuff," Ben breathed, "but *this* . . ."

"This *what*?" Justin asked. He took a step closer, his dark eyebrows slanted in disbelief.

Dr. Moore cleared his throat. "For those of you unfamiliar with the normal insides of a human being, this heart has been cooked. All the way through. See here?" With the tip of his blade he flicked at a dark object that seemed to pull free from the heart itself. "That's a clot. The clot is baked through."

They were silent then. Only the water burbled in reply. The refrigerator hummed, the fluorescent lights buzzed overhead, like night sounds outside her window. It was as if the room itself were holding its breath as everyone waited for Moore to speak again. But it was her father who broke the silence.

"How is that possible?" Patrick demanded.

Dr. Moore planted his legs a step apart, like fence

posts, rooting his top-heavy body to the floor. "I don't have an answer to that question, Coroner. Perhaps he was subjected to a fire elsewhere and was then moved." Moore's face had turned dark, angry, and Cameryn guessed it was because he didn't like to not know the answers. The body was his domain, yet in this case he seemed to understand nothing. "He could have been moved," Moore said again.

"But he was holding his sheet," Cameryn protested. "He died in that bed. He had the sheet clutched in his hand. How could someone pose a person like that?"

"That was only conjecture, Miss Mahoney. My job is to tell you what happened to the decedent medically."

"So you're saying it's murder?" the sheriff asked. His glasses, reflecting light, obscured his eyes.

"At this point, any opinion would be premature," said Moore. "You should know that."

The answer did not seem good enough for Justin. He was pacing behind them, his boots clunking against tile, his head shaking back and forth as he spoke. "What I don't get is how can there be a fire hot enough to cook someone, but not affect the skin? You're the expert, Dr. Moore, but it seems like our vic's outsides aren't burned while his insides are. That's backwards, right?"

"Yes, Deputy, that's backwards. At this point, it appears this man died contrary to every single known burn case on record. But if it was a fire that killed him, there will be smoke in his lungs. I'll be very interested to see what's inside *them*. Let us proceed."

Ben took the heart and weighed it. "Three hundred sixty grams," he said as Patrick dutifully recorded the number on a form. "Normal weight," Ben muttered. "That's the only normal part in this whole thing."

The heart was then dipped in the water and sectioned off for various tests, after which Ben placed it into a Hefty garbage bag with yellow drawstrings bright as ribbons. Cameryn knew that the Hefty bag, once filled with organs, would be deposited back into Mr. Oakes before he was sewed up again. There was nothing romantic in the way a body's insides were transported to the funeral home.

Dr. Moore reached back into the chest and pulled back a lung, slicing it free from the trachea. He then carried it to a cart already laid out with a terry-cloth towel as Ben brought a tube that poured a small stream of water. Dampening the towel, Dr. Moore laid the lung against the wet surface. Then, picking up what looked to be a regular bread knife, he sliced the lung in two and flipped it open like a book, rubbing his hand over the exposed surface. The others crowded around to watch.

"No smoke," Dr. Moore pronounced. "There is no evidence of smoke inhalation, which I would have expected to see if he died by fire, at least in the upper lung. I'll have to run a slide to be sure, but to the naked eye the lungs look clean." He pushed his finger into various points of the tissue, shaking his head in disbelief. "The upper lobe is hard, but the bottom is less so," he said. "There is variegation in the color, too. Brown at the top, more red at the bottom."

"So what about the lung itself?" Sheriff Jacobs pressed. "Is it . . . ?"

Moore gave a terse nod. "Cooked. At least the upper portion. And before you ask, I have absolutely no idea. Let me pull the other lung and get a look. Ben, you forgot my music. I need it to help me focus. At this point I feel like I'm in an episode of *The Twilight Zone*."

Ben sighed as he pulled off his gloves. Flipping through a stack of CDs, he pulled out one and, grinning wickedly, popped it into the CD player. "An oldie but a goodie," he said as hard-rock strains of guitar filled the room.

Dr. Moore's eyebrows disappeared into his hairline as he barked, "What is *that*?"

"*Jesus Christ, Superstar*," Ben said.

"I want opera."

"It is opera. *Rock* opera. There's a line in here that I think's just right for the occasion, so I'll tell you when we get to it. Come on, Dr. Moore, we all need to liven up in here. What we need is some tempo."

Dr. Moore, apparently consumed by more important matters, waved his hand dismissively. "Next time it's

Wagner," he ordered as he removed the right lung, which was bigger than the left, and balanced it in his hand. "I'd say a thousand grams," he told Ben. "When you weigh it, let me know if I'm close." This time he used a pair of scissors to cut through the bronchia, which looked to Cameryn like one-inch tubing. The inevitable verdict was pronounced next. "This one," he said, "is cooked, too. I'll take a section for a fixed slide."

The doctor worked his way down. Organ by organ, Brad Oakes was gutted until only his scooped-out torso remained, as hollow as deer carcasses she'd seen hung at the slaughterhouse outside of town. "Do you know what dissection method I am using here, Miss Mahoney?" Dr. Moore asked.

"The Virchow method."

"Correct. Virchow goes organ by organ, opposed to the Rokitansky method, where the body organs are removed all at once and dissected on the table. Students usually learn Rokitansky first. . . ."

"Why?" Cameryn asked.

"Because the organs will still have the same rela- tionships to one another they had in the body. But the Virchow method is more effective. I'm impressed you knew that."

Cameryn nodded, acknowledging his compliment. As Dr. Moore sliced, sectioned, and weighed the bowels, Brad Oakes's face was still hidden by the triangle of flesh. Gently, Cameryn pulled it away, folding it back onto the chest, exposing the face.

Deliberately, she refused to look at the voids where his eyes had been; instead, she trained her eyes on the folds of his ears, at the crease beneath his lobes and the hair gently curling around it. She'd never realized there was gray mixed with the blond, like a spider's web in yellow grass. Lower down, golden chest hairs spiraled up to his clavicles like tiny springs. His neck had lines on it she hadn't noticed before, human tree rings to mark his age. She looked past his protruding tongue to something unchanged—his nose, a bit too big for his face but strong-looking, the kind of nose you saw in portraits of founding fathers. Hairs bristled from the edge of his nostrils. *He forgot to trim them,* she thought, wondering if the funeral home would fix it until she stopped herself from thinking such stupid thoughts. The man was dead. Who cared anymore? Who would he impress now?

She leaned closer. The strange smell, that she now knew was from his cooked flesh, almost overwhelmed her. "I wish you could tell me what happened to you," she whispered so softly her lips barely moved. "I'm sorry this is how your life ended, Mr. Oakes. You taught me so much. I . . . I already miss you. I wish you could hear me."

Cameryn waited, wanting to feel something of him coming into her, his spirit, perhaps, vibrating a thought into her mind. Lyric claimed that the ghosts of the departed were all around, watching their bodies when they died and sometimes getting confused about whether they were actually dead. She said sensitive people were able to channel the thoughts of the dead into their minds, enabling them to speak once more. But Cameryn only half-believed this. The priest told her a different story, that upon death the soul soared with the angels. Whichever way was right, the soul of her teacher was no longer here. Just his shell, empty, exposed.

"Cameryn," Ben said gently. "We need to do his head now. Are you ready?"

"Sure."

Straightening, she looked at him. Ben had a mask on, a blue one with a piece of duct tape over the bridge. He placed Mr. Oakes's neck on a head block, which raised it almost five inches. With a precision cut, Ben sliced through the scalp in an incision that reached from one of Oakes's ears to the other. He pulled the top of the scalp forward, slicing away the temporalis muscle, and then stretched the scalp, hair and all, folding it over the front of the teacher's face, which he then tucked beneath his chin. Mr. Oakes's face was once again hidden as though it had been erased. Veins snaked along the exposed scalp like tiny branches.

"This is a bone saw," Ben said, holding up a handheld instrument. "It's a Stryker. The interesting thing about these is they don't oscillate—these are the same saws that they used to cut off casts with. Only they call them an autopsy saw and double the price. You might want to put on a mask now, Cammie. This kicks up a bit of bone dust, and I don't want you breathing that. Take this one."

He handed her one made of blue paper, with a white reinforced edge. Tying it on, she watched in fascination as Ben pressed the whirring blade in the middle of Oakes's brow bone. The saw made a grinding sound as Ben gripped the skull with his left hand and cut all the way to where an ear had once been. Then, returning to the middle, he cut to the other ear in a horizontal line. Repositioning the saw, he cut from the end point all the way across the top of her teacher's head, ending at the other ear, stopping in the middle of the line to make a small notch.

"What's that for?" she asked.

"Makes it easier when I got to put the skull back on. It's like carving a notch in the top of a pumpkin, you know?"

Next, he inserted what looked to be a flat screwdriver into the groove cut into the bowline. When he twisted hard, the skull made a sickening crack. Repeating the process lower down, Ben wrenched the screwdriver again, and this time the skull popped off in his hand. He removed the skull cap and bent close.

All she could see over the top of the mask was his eyes going wide. "Dr. Moore, you better take a look at this!" he cried.

The brain had exploded. As in the eyes, the water in the brain must have expanded in the skull until the tissue burst, leaving a mess inside resembling hamburger.

"My God," Dr. Moore said, his voice grim. "This is sci-fi. This isn't medicine as I know it."

They stood, staring numbly, as the music pounded in the background. "Could you turn that down, Ben? It's giving me a headache!" Moore told him.

"Sure thing. But wait—here's the line I wanted you all to hear."

A rocker's raspy voice filled the autopsy suite in a sad melody with words that drilled into Cameryn. The man sang: "To conquer death you only have to die—you only have to die."

Chapter Eight

THE SMELL OF cigarette smoke wafted up to where Cameryn sat, making her eyes water, while Adam, head back and nostrils flared, drank it in like nectar. On the main floor where Cameryn and Adam and Lyric sat, Durango's family-friendly restaurant called Scoot 'n Blues boasted a smoke-free environment. It was a meaningless claim. In the netherworld below, Scoot 'n Blues's sister organization, The Sidecar Jazz Lounge, pulsed with energy and gave off the effluence of adult vices, which in turn drifted up the open stairwell separating the two floors. And although she'd never before wished it, tonight Cameryn longed to be downstairs in the Jazz Lounge, drinking and blotting out the day in blissful oblivion.

She knew she was lousy company tonight, but after

all, she hadn't wanted to come here. Back at the medical examiner's building while she was still scrubbing up after the autopsy, Lyric had phoned with an offer for dinner, which Cameryn's father, hovering nearby, overheard.

"I want us to have a personal tribute for Mr. Oakes," Lyric had said. "Adam and I are already at S&B's and we have a table, so no excuses. We'll wait for you. I really think we need to do this. The three of us should honor him."

Cameryn had been in the middle of refusing when her father intervened. "It'll do you good, Cammie," he'd insisted. "Your friends have made a trip all the way down to Durango just for you. I'll drop you off at the S&B. Come on, it's Saturday night. You've been at it all day. Go! Eat! Try to get death out of your head."

But she couldn't. Sitting here in the over-plumped vinyl booth, she could only visualize images of her teacher's empty skull and of the Hefty bag sewn back into his gutted torso. And with all that cutting, there were still no answers. The line on the death certificate stating cause of death contained one word: unknown.

So far, the conversation had come in fits and starts, with Cameryn barely contributing more than a monosyllabic reply. She almost felt sorry for Lyric and Adam as they tried to draw her out, but then again, she felt too tired to help them.

"This is a cool place," Adam said, craning his neck. "Retro, with a touch of the modern. Service is painfully slow, though. Not like how it is at the Grand."

"Thanks. But this place is really busy and it's a Saturday night," Cameryn replied.

Adam's fingers drummed along the edge of the tabletop. "I just wish they'd let me light up." He pulled a pack of Marlboros from his shirt pocket and held it under his nose, sniffing deeply. "I could really use a smoke right now. It makes no sense to designate one room nonsmoking when they're going at it like chimneys ten feet below us and we're sitting next to an open stairwell."

"You're right," Lyric agreed.

"I mean, do they think the sign itself has some magical powers? Like the air wouldn't dare blow past it?"

Rousing herself, Cameryn said, "Secondhand smoke is bad enough, Adam. You know those things will kill you. And seeing as I just came from slicing up someone's insides, I can assure you that you don't want to die."

"I don't, but you also got to remember that good health is just the slowest possible means to arrive at the inevitable end." Adam put his cigarettes back into his pocket, patting them affectionately. "I mean, the harsh reality is we're all destined for the grave. Besides, you know that the spirit lives on. I wouldn't be surprised if Oakes was hovering over us right now, watching us from the ceiling."

"Oh, please," Cameryn groaned, "it's been *way* too long a day for a bunch of woo-woo theories on the afterlife. I am *so* not in the mood."

"Whoa, man, where did *that* come from?" Adam asked. He plowed his thin fingers through his sooty hair, saying, "You got to know death is part of life."

"Yeah, but it's also blood and brains and . . . loss." Cameryn shook her head. "I'm sorry, maybe I shouldn't have gone out with you guys tonight. I'm not very good company right now. Obviously."

The jazz band fired up, a thumping old-timey rendition of "Maple Leaf Rag," which made Lyric almost shout to be heard. Her eyes, rimmed in cobalt blue, had widened in sympathy. "That's exactly why you need your friends," she cried, patting Cameryn with a ring-adorned hand. "That's the reason we came all the way down here. To help you through your god-awful day. Be you happy or sad—whatever your emotion is, you're entitled to feel it. You know you can be real with us."

"Thank you, Dr. Phil."

Lyric retracted her hand. "What is with you tonight, Cammie? We're only trying to help."

That was another thing bothering her, Cameryn realized, although she didn't want to admit it. Her best friend was now one half of a couple. The realization that their longtime friendship of two had made way to include another person—rearranging the way things had been done since grade school—had Cameryn feeling left out. Adam, Silverton's weird loner in black, had become part of their friendship equation. It was no longer just loud, mystic Lyric and scientific Cameryn against the world. The two had become three.

She stole a glance at Adam, at his cheeks, thin to the point of hollowness, and his pale eyes that looked bland while the mind behind them clicked and whirred. It wasn't that she begrudged her best friend having a boyfriend, exactly—though Lyric had never had a guy before. No, it was the fact that lately, everywhere Cameryn turned, her life seemed to shift beneath her, changing the way drifts of snow could rise and melt in a single day in the mountains around Silverton. She realized she wanted things to stay the same. Even more, she wanted her old life back, and that was impossible.

"Are you ready to order?"

Cameryn looked up to see a college-aged man with blond dreadlocks, wearing a Scoot 'n Blues polo shirt hanging loosely over khakis, the outfit at odds with his Rastafarian hair that sprouted from his head in fuzzy coils.

"I'll have a cheeseburger," Cameryn began, but Lyric cut her off.

"I'm sorry, we're waiting for someone else," she said, shooting a sly smile Cameryn's way. "Can we just have two iced teas and a Diet Coke while we wait? And another place setting, please." Lyric didn't need to ask if Cameryn wanted the Diet Coke. It was Cameryn's standing order.

"Not a problem," the server said, and disappeared.

For a moment, despite her dark mood, Cameryn felt a stirring of interest because this was unexpected. "What's up?" she asked. "Who else is coming tonight?"

"Just wait," Lyric whispered, leaning in conspiratorially. "We've got a surprise for you."

Cameryn felt her blood freeze. "Is it . . . is it Hannah?"

"No, no, no," Lyric assured her, leaning back into the booth. "Nothing so dramatic. This surprise is just for fun. Fun—remember the concept? I guarantee this person will cheer you right up." She and Adam exchanged knowing glances.

"Come on, tell me!"

"Sorry. No can do. Patience, young lady. And try to lighten your mood, will you? You're as much fun as a root canal." Lyric's round shoulders moved in time to the sliding trombone solo of "Mood Indigo," rising from below.

Contrasting with the gray of November, Lyric wore her trademark loud color, this time electric yellow. The blue tips she used to have on the ends of her hair had been extended to the roots; now her whole head seemed to glow blue, a stark contrast to the vivid yellow and the deep red of her pants, the thick black work boots that laced up the front, the chunky red and yellow bracelets.

Adam, though, seemed to fade into the surroundings. Scoot 'n Blues's dim interior accentuated the contrast between his skin and his black hair and clothes so that at times his hands and face appeared disembodied.

Cameryn felt a pang of guilt because the two of them were trying so hard to help her and she'd repaid them by being a total witch. She had to pull it together. She had to make an effort.

"You're smiling. What are you smiling at?" Lyric wanted to know.

"Nothing. Just an observation."

"What is it? Come on, spill!"

"It's just, you know, with that red-and-yellow outfit of yours along with that blue-green hair, I'm thinking your look says 'traffic light.'"

"That's harsh," Adam said, but Lyric laughed.

"Yeah," she agreed. "Well, John Denver called and said he wants *his* look back from you."

"John Denver is dead—"

"So's his fashion, flannel-girl," Lyric fired back.

"I'm not *wearing* flannel."

"But you own it, don't you? I've seen it in your closet. Admitting your problem is the first step, Cammie."

Adam's pale eyes widened. He didn't understand the way they teased, didn't know that joking was the way the two of them got their rhythm back. Cameryn felt her insides unkink as she sipped her water, deciding that her father had been right after all. She needed this, to be back among the living. The music, the explosion of laughter from an adjoining table, even the wafting smoke rising like incense, all were the siren song of the undead.

The server brought their drinks, putting them down carefully on paper coasters, then setting a place next to Cameryn for the nonexistent guest. When he was gone, Lyric raised her iced tea to the ceiling and cleared her throat. Her face became serious, her tone more solemn, as she said, "One of the reasons I wanted to come to Scoot 'n Blues is because I remember the way Mr. Oakes loved jazz and blues. So I thought we should raise a glass and remember the man. To Mr. Oakes," she said, lifting the tea higher. "May he rest in peace."

"To Mr. Oakes," Adam and Cameryn echoed. They clinked their sweating glasses together and drank, while Cameryn added a silent prayer of her own.

"What about me?" someone behind her said. "Don't I get to toast?"

Cameryn whirled in her seat to see a familiar face. Kyle O'Neil, wearing jeans and a green-and-gold CSU sweatshirt, stood right behind her. "Sorry I couldn't get here earlier," he apologized. "I came as soon as I could. Do you mind, Cameryn?"

Not waiting for a reply, he slid into the booth next to Cameryn, so close his thigh touched hers. She could feel the hardness of his muscle beneath the denim, could smell the spice of his deodorant as his arm raised and lowered when he settled in close to her. Scooting over, she noticed that his blond hair looked like honey in the light. A stubble had appeared above his upper lip and on his chin, but of deep amber, more the color of his lashes.

"What are you doing here?" Cameryn asked.

"I met up with Lyric at the Steamin' Bean earlier today, and we started talking. She said you all were going to have an informal tribute to Brad and, well, since Brad was so important to me, I asked if I could come. She said yes, and here I am. So, could I do a toast?" Kyle asked, looking from face to face.

"Go for it," Adam said.

"Lyric, can I steal your water?"

"Sure." Lyric shoved her glass across the table.

And then, in a voice that sound strangely rehearsed, but not without effect, Kyle closed his eyes, his long lashes coming together against his high cheekbones. Keeping his lids shut, he raised his glass and said, "Unlike the mythic phoenix, the body turns particles of earth, and earth remains, and yet the soul unburdened soars into the heavens"—he faltered—"to become the dust of stars." Kyle's voice was soft, barely audible over the throbbing music. He opened his eyes but didn't look at any of them. Instead, his gaze searched the ceiling, and in a thickened voice, he said, "Brad—Mr. Oakes—you taught us to soar. May God be with you, now and forever."

Clinking glasses, they drank, Cameryn and Lyric sipping, Adam and Kyle chugging theirs.

"Wow," Lyric said as she set down her glass. "That was awesome, Kyle. Did you make that up?"

Kyle shook his head. "No, that's Shane Kearney. Oakes made us memorize poems, and that was one I did in class. Kearney's Irish, like me. But his writings are more like inspirational poetry."

"Really?" Lyric said. "Did you know Cameryn's Irish, too?"

Kyle's amber eyes slid over to hers. "I figured. With a name like Mahoney, it's a pretty safe bet."

Cameryn looked away, out the overly bright, neon-lit window. She had an idea that this was all part of the plan that Lyric and Adam must have cooked up in Silverton. The tribute to their teacher, the nightclub atmosphere of Scoot 'n Blues, the way Kyle rounded out the foursome—it all smacked of a lonely-heart intervention. Part of her wanted to reach out and throttle her friend, but at the same time she asked herself if she needed a breath mint. There was no real harm in spending some time with Kyle. She'd already told him her life was too busy to include another person, and that much was still true. And yet . . . she had to admit he was good-looking. And interesting. She supposed she could at least try to be civil. Which meant she should try to join the conversation.

"Mr. Oakes was one-quarter Irish," Cameryn ventured.

"He came to our church off and on. I'll bet they'll do a Mass for him there."

"Brad went to St. Pat's? I didn't know that."

"Twice a year. Easter and Christmas—you know, the Lily and Poinsettia Club. A little Communion, a sprinkle of holy water, maybe a quick confession, and you're good for a year. My mammaw calls it fire insurance."

"My family's Catholic, too, but we really never go," Kyle said. "My dad doesn't like organized religion."

"Lucky. My grandmother's first-generation Irish. I'm never allowed to miss unless I'm so sick I'm hovering near death. But even though I go all the time and say the rosary, she's pretty convinced I'm going to hell, I think."

Adam shook his head. "That's because you want to be a forensic pathologist instead of a real doctor."

She could feel the vibration of the bass guitar on the soles of her feet, tiny buzzes of electricity that traveled up her legs. Glancing upward, through the hazy film of menthol smoke that gave the light inside a blue cast, she stated with annoyance, "Once again, Adam, I would like to remind you and everyone else on the planet that a forensic pathologist *is* a real doctor. I'll do the exact same things as a regular doctor, except too late."

A shout of laughter erupted from Kyle, and Cameryn felt herself flush. He thought she was funny. She'd never felt witty before, especially in the company of someone like Kyle O'Neil. Lyric was sending messages with her eyes, that she knew this was a good idea and that Cameryn owed her big-time. *All right, all right,* Cameryn telegraphed back, *he's not so bad and I won't kill you, after all.*

The night passed in a blur. The four of them told stories of Mr. Oakes, both funny and sad, and more than once Lyric's eyes welled with tears as they raised their glasses in remembrance of their teacher. Somewhere along the line Cameryn had felt lighter inside. The pain had lessened, if only by the smallest of weights, like feathers being lifted off a scale. At one point she actually found herself laughing—Kyle had told a joke, touching the top of her arm at the moment he delivered the punch line, and she sensed a kind of energy radiating from him, through those fingertips. The feeling surprised her. She'd grown used to sending her emotions underground, and here they were, like shoots of grass breaking through concrete.

Later, as she sipped her Diet Coke, she noticed the little things about him, like the way Kyle talked to Adam as an equal, even though Adam was a weird goth with a reputation, and how Kyle listened to everything Lyric said, as if she was as important as any cheerleader. *He's nice,* she realized. *Not at all what I expected.* When it was time to go, Kyle surprised them all by paying the entire bill.

"It's not a problem, I'll just use my card," he said. "Really, you guys, this has been great."

"You have your own credit card?" Cameryn marveled.

"It's technically my dad's. He's not around that much."

"What about your mom?"

"She's out in California. Has been for about a year." He didn't elaborate, and Cameryn didn't ask. Absent mothers—another link in the chain forged between them.

Finally, after stretching her arms over her head, Lyric yawned and stood. "We've got to get going," she said. "Come on, Adam. We still got all that stuff to do and it's getting late."

"Wait a minute, what about me?" Cameryn protested. "You're supposed to take me back to Silverton!"

Lyric looked at her with a perplexed expression that didn't fool Cameryn at all. This, too, she realized, had been part of the plan.

"Oh, Cammie, the thing is Adam and I were going to shop at the Durango Mall first," she said. "You could come with us, I guess."

"Hey, a ride's not a problem," Kyle said, jumping in. "I can do it. Would that be all right with you, Cameryn? I'm a very safe driver." He held up two fingers pressed together and said, "Eagle Scout, remember?"

"I don't want to put you out or anything."

"What are you talking about—we're going to the same town! So Adam, you and Lyric go ahead, and I'll get Cameryn home. But you guys had better hurry. The mall's closing soon."

"Right," said Adam.

As they settled it between the three of them, Cameryn felt as though she were lying back in the water, for once floating along in life's stream instead of fighting its current. Tonight she didn't have to make decisions that revolved around human remains. Instead she could be seventeen again and let life just . . . happen. She found herself being helped into her jacket by Kyle before he shrugged on his own snowboarder's coat he'd left on the hook at the front. With his hand on the small of her back, he gently guided her out of Scoot 'n Blues, protective and in control.

"You ready?" he asked.

"Yeah. I guess I am."

He smiled at her, his teeth flashing in the neon sign's light. "I was thinking of making one stop first. It's in Silverton and it'll only take a minute. The place is special to me and I'd—I'd like to take you there. If you don't mind."

"I don't mind," she said, surprised to realize she didn't. "I'm up for anything. So where are we going?"

He was looking at her in a strange way, his eyes intense. There was a pause. His mouth moved as if to say something, but then he shook his head, as if suddenly thinking the better of it.

"You know what?" he said. "Maybe we'd better not. For a minute it seemed like a good idea, but . . ."

"Okay, now you *have* to tell me."

Again the pause. "I don't want to scare you."

Cameryn felt a prick of apprehension, which she quickly dismissed. It was obvious he was joking. Cocking her head, she said, "Ah, but I don't scare easy." She pushed against him, playful. "Go ahead. Hit me with it. I'm not afraid, Kyle. I mean, you're a Boy Scout, after all. Where is this place?"

Just then a car went by, kicking gray slush into the gutter. Kyle watched as it disappeared down Durango's Main Street.

"Kyle?"

"You'll think I'm crazy."

"How crazy can a Boy Scout be?"

His face came close to hers, and once again she saw the gold flecks of his eyes. So soft it was almost a whisper, he said, "I want to take you to the cemetery."

Chapter Nine

"EVER SEE HILLSIDE Cemetery in the moonlight?" Kyle asked her. He'd parked his car, an older model Subaru, outside the cemetery road, an unpaved lane that looped around the foothill of Storm Mountain like the edge of a trumpet shell. On the drive up he'd been easy to talk to, and Cameryn, still relaxed, had floated in the current of Kyle's attention. His voice quieted thoughts of her mother and erased the picture of Mr. Oakes that had burned her mind. During the drive, she'd done little of the talking. Kyle had spoken of football, being an Eagle Scout, his commitment to aim high, the pressure he felt to make the perfect 4.0, and his need to earn scholarship money.

"You shouldn't have paid for dinner," she'd said.

"Hey, my old man gives me an allowance and I never

spend it. It was good to finally put the card to some use other than groceries. Besides, this was a tough day. For both of us." Seconds later he added unexpectedly, "My dad wasn't a fan of Mr. Oakes."

"He wasn't?" Cameryn asked, surprised. "How come?"

"I don't know." He shrugged, then apparently thinking better of it, said, "That's not true. I *do* know. I guess it's because I liked Brad . . . better than my own father."

She stared at Kyle, gaping.

"I know that sounds bad. But my dad's not been around much and I've been left on my own. Not that I've minded. But there've been times when his disappearing act sucked. Like when I was made an Eagle Scout—parents usually go all out for their kids when they get that far. But my dad did nothing. Brad's the one who put the whole ceremony together, with food and everything. And instead of being grateful, my dad got pissed."

"Why?"

"Because he told Brad it wasn't his job. Which was so much crap—Brad only stepped up because my dad checked out. Later, my dad said I worship at the throne of Mr. Oakes. He called him 'Saint Brad.'" Kyle snorted softly. "One of the few times my old man was right. Mr. Oakes *was* a saint." He turned toward her with sudden intensity. "Cameryn, I really want to know what happened to Mr. Oakes. What did you find out in the autopsy? Can you tell me?"

She hesitated. Part of her wanted to go over everything she'd seen, but she knew it was unethical. When she told him she couldn't talk about the case, he nodded, then fell silent. She liked that he didn't press.

Now, as the moon drenched the inside of his car, silvering the dashboard, he leaned closer, conspiratorially. "We'll have to stay quiet," he said, and his voice was hushed. "If the neighbors hear us they might call the cops. See the sign? The cemetery's closed at night."

"When did that happen?"

"There was some trouble a while back. A couple of guys on the team had some beers, got a little crazy, and knocked over a few headstones. That chain's supposed to keep out the partiers. So how do you feel about breaking the law?"

"Usually I'm a straight-arrow kind of girl. But that's a pretty dumb law."

"My feelings exactly. Follow the rules, except when they make no sense."

"I thought you were a Boy Scout," she said.

"I see myself as a thinking man. So let's do it."

When Cameryn stepped outside, she realized how cold it had become. Her coat wasn't heavy enough for a trip among the headstones. She looked at the chain barring their way and the flimsy, hand-painted sign listing hours, and pictured Justin roaring up to the cemetery with his red-and-blue lights flashing like a mirrored ball.

Hesitant, she asked, "Tell me again why we're here?"

"Because I want to show you something."

"Why not show me where you live instead? I bet you've got central heating in your house," she kidded, "which is a big plus."

She sensed, rather than saw, Kyle stiffen. "My dad's home now, so I don't want to take you there. The cemetery is a place where we can be alone. If you don't count all the dead people." Tugging on her coat sleeve, he said, "Come on, I didn't figure you to be a wimp."

"You think I'm *wimpy*?"

"I'm just calling it like I see it."

And then it was too late. Throwing the veil of her hair over her shoulder, she said, "I'm all over it."

Cameryn easily stepped over the chain, her footsteps crunching in the gravel road as she began to hike along the path. She looked back to see if anyone had noticed the two of them, but all seemed quiet. A few neighboring houses, the kind made from logs with pitched green roofs, seemed to stand guard. Lights blazed inside them, but she saw no faces blotting out the windows.

"See? Piece of cake," Kyle told her.

Twenty feet up the path, the actual graves started. The moon was three-quarters full, and its light filtered through the headstones, casting eerie shadows against bright patches of snow. She noticed tattered cobwebs moving gently in the air, catching the silvery light like lace. As they trudged farther and farther along the gravel path, Cameryn felt her toes growing numb. Kyle, who walked one step ahead, didn't seem bothered by the cold.

"I see dead people," he said hoarsely.

"I see stupid people," she countered. "You and me."

The cemetery was old, and it was big, and wherever it was he was taking her must be located in the farthest possible corner. When her feet felt like blocks of ice she cried, "Kyle, where are we going?"

He stopped and turned. "What? Seriously, are you scared?"

"No, I'm *cold*. Kyle, I'm freezing." Hugging her sides, her bare hands tucked beneath her armpits, Cameryn danced while she talked. She could see him clearly in the almost-full moon, and its radiance had a dual effect: it glanced off his hair while creating planes of light and dark on his face. His eyes, lost in shadow, were impossible to read.

"How about if *I* keep you warm?" he asked.

Her heart skipped inside her chest. "What?"

"I'm offering you my coat. Boy Scout, remember?" He unzipped his parka and draped it around her, even as she protested. "Don't worry about me," he said. "I'm cold-blooded."

The inside of his coat felt warm, and it smelled good. A hint of wood smoke clung to it. Pulling it tight, she felt her blood flow again. He was standing very close. After he'd given her his coat, he hadn't moved away. Then, touching her cheek with his hand, he said, "Your skin is like ice, Cammie. Maybe we should go back."

"Maybe," she said, and turned her face toward his ever so slightly.

Kyle's breath made puffs of steam. "Whatever you want," he said.

Her practical side told her to go home. But she had to admit she liked the hint of danger in this. She, who almost always followed the rules, was bending them with a boy. Her father would not approve. Her mammaw would be scandalized. But above all this, she'd just discovered an important truth: that when her body was in motion, her mind was at rest. As she'd wound her way among the headstones, she found that it wasn't only her feet that went numb. She liked this—the not thinking. It felt good.

"I'm not a quitter, especially after I've pinched a warm coat," she told him. "And by the way, I don't think you meant to say 'cold-blooded.' That's like a reptile. A lizard would die in this cold."

He laughed, and she liked the sound of it, deep and masculine. "I stand corrected. Hanging out with you is like dating a teacher."

"Gee. Thanks." But his words made her pulse beat faster. He'd said the word "date."

"*That* sounded sarcastic."

"Really?" She grinned. "You think I'm sarcastic? Watch me pretend to care."

"Oh, you're funny, Cameryn. I like that. I like someone I can laugh with. And since I am a Scout and I have pledged to help those in need, I'll now selflessly help keep your fingers from freezing off. It's the least I can do."

He held out his hand. Timidly, she placed hers in his. Inside, her mind was awake again. Now it was screaming, *Too fast, too fast, too fast!*

"Your hand is so small," he murmured. "It's like a kid's." His felt surprisingly warm as it closed around hers. "Let's move out," he told her.

Leaning back as if on a rope tow, Cameryn raced after him through the graves, weaving around headstones as though they were buoys in water. It was fun to run this way. She felt the last of the day's horror fading away as her feet churned through patches of snow.

She'd always thought this was the place she'd like to be buried. Unlike most cemeteries, Hillside, as its name implied, had been carved into a foothill. Layered like a wedding cake, with snow instead of frosting and headstones in place of confectioners' roses, it had a history of miners and prostitutes, mayors and madams. They wove around a mass grave from the flu epidemic of 1918. Farther along was a mausoleum boasting a

Russian princess, a woman named Edna Harris who'd been embroiled in a bizarre love triangle that included the man who became the chief architect of Silverton. Silverton had always been strangely proud of its scandalous past, and Cameryn was proud, too. She'd like to spend her afterlife talking with such an eclectic group of corpses.

They raced past plots where whole families were buried behind spiked fences, hemming them in like a prizefighter's ring. Some, like the family she streaked by on her right, seemed cheerful in death: moonlight revealed their headstones decorated with beads and glass trinkets, whirligigs, and Hawaiian leis. Other graves, though, told a different story—headstones erased by a century of harsh weather, or tipped over by gravity and neglect. It saddened her to realize that even under the cover of night, she could easily tell who'd been forgotten.

"We made it," he said. "Come on, have a seat."

He sat down on a wooden bench positioned to face a tombstone. Cameryn squeezed in beside him. There was barely room for the two of them, so their legs pressed together again, as they had in the restaurant, but this time she couldn't move away. And she wasn't sure she would have, even if there'd been miles of room.

"Okay," she said, "what am I supposed to see?"

Kyle hesitated. "There," he said, pointing to a headstone.

It was an old-fashioned grave marker made to look like the pages of an open Bible. Carved on the granite were letters denoting someone's death. Since it was too dark for Cameryn to read, she asked, "What does it say?"

"It says, 'Mary Fitzgerald, 1966. My anam cara.'"

"Who's Mary Fitzgerald?" she asked. "And what's an *anam cara*?"

"She's my grandmother. My mother's mother."

"Oh. I'm sorry."

"Don't be. *Anam cara* is Gaelic. *Anam* is the Irish word for 'soul' and *cara* is the word for 'friend.' So it means 'soul friend.' That was my grandfather's name for her."

When he put his hand on her arm, she could barely feel it through the coat's thick padding, but her nerves began to prickle beneath her skin. He was leaning in, nearer. *Too fast, too fast, too fast,* raced through her mind again.

"Aren't you cold?" she asked.

"I'm warmer, now that we're close."

"I can give you back your coat."

"You keep it."

The bench was at the edge of the cemetery, next to the tree line, and beyond Kyle's head she could see branches touching branches, holding hands in moonlight, as if they could keep back the invisible legion of trees covered in shadow. Then she had a crazy thought: She'd been like those trees—not the ones on the edge that were easily seen, but the ones behind, hiding in that vast, unseen, evergreen army marching up the mountainside. She'd been hiding from her mammaw and her father and, most frightening of all, from herself. And here was Kyle, wanting to draw her out.

"*Anam cara*," she said, turning the words in her mouth. "I like that."

She felt his hand stroking hers. "I was . . . I was thinking that you and me . . . we have something like that now. After today, I think we have *anam cara*."

"We do?"

"We've got a link to each other. I mean, we're the only kids in school who saw Brad in that room. There's no one else who can understand it. Just you . . . and I."

"Why did you bring me here?" she asked softly.

"Honestly?"

"Yes." Her one word made a single puff in the cold air.

"So we could be alone. Where no one could see. And so I could do this."

And then he was kissing her, kissing the girl who'd hardly ever been kissed. She could feel the whiskers of his upper lip against her own, rough as sandpaper, and beneath that she could taste the lingering taste of chocolate mint. His hands caressed her neck as he pulled her closer, but then his tongue entered her mouth and she pulled away.

"Don't," she said.

He didn't seem to hear. He kissed her again.

"Wait," she said, louder this time. "I can't."

Now he did hear. Pulling back from her, she saw he was frowning, but puzzled, too.

"What's the matter? Are you going with someone?"

"Going? No. That's not it." A picture of Justin flashed through her mind, but she quickly dismissed his image. Her father said Justin was too old for her, and maybe that was true. But more importantly, Justin had already seen inside her head. He understood her weaknesses. No, if she ever began a relationship, she'd want to be able to show herself in the most flattering light, then slowly reveal herself. She couldn't do that with Justin. He already knew too much.

"If it's not another guy, then . . . why?"

"Kyle, I just can't. I just can't get involved with some-one—anyone—right now."

"Why not?"

How could she tell him about Hannah, and how she couldn't squeeze out one more drop of herself for anyone? That her life was already too difficult and was about to get more so. She felt herself fading back, away from the lights and into the trees, but Kyle was holding on to her tightly.

"If there's not another guy then there must be a reason."

"My life is . . . complicated."

"Whose isn't?"

"Really? What's complicated about yours?" she challenged.

"You really want to know?"

Cameryn nodded.

"Okay, then I'll make a deal. I'll tell you my story if you tell me yours. But it has to be the truth. *Anam cara.* All right?"

She thought only a moment before saying, "All right." Silently, she added that she could edit her own story, airbrush it until it became whatever she wanted. For her, the deal was struck because she was curious about Kyle. Kyle O'Neil, the boy no girl in Silverton could get, who was sitting beneath a frosted sky wanting to kiss her.

"All right," he began. "But first, I don't want you reporting what I say to Lyric or any of the other girls you run around with. I know how girls are."

"Hello, you're sounding sexist. Not okay!"

"No, no, no, that's not what I meant. I'm just asking—do you keep secrets?"

Now Cameryn smiled. "More than you'll ever know. So tell me."

Resting his head on the back of the bench, Kyle looked up at the stars. Then he began to tell his story, and as he did, Cameryn started to see the pattern of his life. Its design surprised her. His mother had gone away with another man, and he hadn't seen her in over two years.

"I get postcards," he said. "Freaking postcards with one line on them. Like that would make everything all right. And then my dad, it's like he left me, too. He drives his trucks from one end of the country to the other, weeks at a time, and he takes our dog Skooch with him. My dad loves that dog—if he had to pick me or Skooch, Skooch'd win. For me, he just deposits cash into my account and then he disappears. But it's really better that way. Two men together can end up killing each other."

"But you always seem so . . . upbeat."

He shrugged. "I do the best I can. I figure attitude is a choice. So Brad . . ." When he said the name, Kyle faltered. "Brad filled the void. He was like a father to me. The point is, everyone, whether you know it or not, has got problems. And the truth is, you never know what's really going on in someone's head."

They sat in silence, until he said, "*Anam cara.* Now you."

Once again the words raced though her head, but *Too fast, too fast, too fast* gave way to *Just feel, don't think, just feel, don't think. No, you can't give in,* she told herself fiercely. *You can't add another person to your life, not when Hannah's coming.* Yet Kyle had shared his own unhappiness with her, and she'd agreed, hadn't she?

Quickly she blurted, "My mother—left me, too. A long time ago. But she's . . . she's . . ."

"She's what?" Kyle murmured.

"No. End of story." Guilt washed over her because she'd been lying for weeks to her father about her tentative contact with her mother. And here in this shadowed place, she'd almost revealed the secret to this stranger. What magic did Kyle possess that had nearly broken through her guard? It was as if she were a snowboarder at the top of a perilous mountain, and he'd gently urged her to slide over the precipice.

Kyle leaned closer and said, "You're cautious. I like that. Other girls . . ." He didn't finish the thought, leaving Cameryn to wonder just how far *other* girls opened up for Kyle. Touching her face, he whispered, "Can I kiss you, just one more time? Then we'll go. I promise."

He bent close, and his kiss was sweeter this time. As light as petals, his lips brushed hers. The beat of her heart would drown out everything, if she let it. Drawing her head onto his chest, tucking his chin on top, he said, "Now I really am getting cold." Through the down of his jacket she could hear his heart thudding like a mallet on wood.

With the kiss, the edge of the snowboard tipped, and then she gave herself a shove and burst into the snow. She was sailing, streaming down the mountainside, and there was no end in sight, the snow burning her skin and eyes, and for once she didn't care. Careening down where there was no trail—that was something she never did, but that was before, when she listened to the objections that always crowded her thoughts. Raising her head, she put her cheek against his, and then, slowly, softly, her lips found his.

She'd always used her brain to navigate through life. Now, perhaps stupidly, perhaps mercifully, she let go.

For the first time in her life, she was flying blind.

Chapter Ten

"SO WE CAN go out after school for a bite to eat," Kyle said. "If you want."

Cameryn's heart brimmed as she nodded. They were walking up the stairs of her venerable old school, the place where she had spent so much of her life both learning and marking time. This Monday morning, though, the building looked different somehow. The brick, which she'd once thought resembled yellowed teeth, now seemed warm, butter-colored. The windows sparkled in the sunrise, reflecting sheets of gold, and the mountain made a perfect backdrop to the school as if holding the building in the cup of its hand.

"I bet a few people are going to be surprised at the two of us," Kyle said.

Nodding, she looked up at him. "Yeah. I mean, it's— we've—been awfully fast."

"Good thing I like speed," he answered, and smiled. His arm draped around her as he tucked her into his side. The blue-and-white letterman jacket, trimmed with academic pins, anchored her; if not for that weight, she felt as though she might float up beyond the rim of pine and straight into the cold November sky. She felt that light, that free.

Kyle stopped and pointed at the flagpole near the front office. "Look! They lowered the flag to half-mast. That's got to be for Brad."

"It's our first day back since he died."

"Yeah. It's going to be a rough day. I'm glad I've got you," he said, squeezing her tight.

"Me, too."

And there it was again—the pang that rose up to drown out her joy. The spasm of guilt. Guilt because she felt so happy when so many bad things marched in formation beside her. Fifty miles away, her teacher's body lay on the funeral home's steel tabletop, prepped and ready for embalming. While Cameryn snuggled beneath Kyle's arm, Mr. Oakes's body would be propped on an incline table to ensure the proper drainage. She knew what came next: Blood from his body would leach out into the Durango sewer system, to be replaced inside Mr. Oakes with a fleshy-pink formaldehyde pumped through tubes inserted at six points: his femoral arteries, the axillaries in his arms, and the carotids in his neck. Cavity-fluid preservative would be poured onto his organs, still left in the garbage bag, and his insides, bag and all, would be sewn into his remains with crude stitches. Mr. Oakes's jaw would be wired shut. All this would happen to what was left of her teacher while Cameryn was filled with a kind of euphoria that told her no matter what, she was alive and Kyle liked her. It wasn't right, but she couldn't help the positive energy radiating from her.

Her enthusiasm hadn't gone unnoticed.

Yesterday morning, while kneeling at St. Patrick's, she'd seen parishioners around her bent with grief. As the priest chanted a prayer for Mr. Oakes, Cameryn's mind was somewhere else. It replayed her kiss in the cemetery and how it had ended with Kyle pulling her to her feet, her neck craning back as he kissed her again and again until she'd told him it was time to go. She remembered the warmth of his cheek as he pressed it next to hers. Savoring this memory, her mind dwelled not on her teacher's death but on her own new life. Something must have shown on her face, because a moment later her mammaw had whispered into her ear, "Stop that smiling. It's unbecoming under the circumstances," and the next words had been a hiss beneath Mammaw's breath: "You're losing your head over a boy when you should be praying for your poor teacher."

"I *am*," she'd whispered back. "Look, I'm saying the rosary." She'd held up the beads, still wrapped around her hand. The crucifix swayed beneath her fist.

"You're not fooling me," her grandmother muttered. "And you're not fooling God."

Lyric had called right after Mass, wanting to know everything that had happened after the restaurant. How long had they kissed Saturday night? Cameryn tried to tell her, but in truth she couldn't remember. Ten minutes? Twenty? She had no idea, because time had melted away as she held on to him beneath the silver moon and the shadow of the graves, and she'd thought how perfect it was, to have something begin where most things ended.

"Just don't move too fast," Lyric warned. "He's a great guy and all, but you're going through a lot right now and maybe you're streaking along with Kyle because you don't want to leave space in your head to think about your mom coming back."

"Don't psychoanalyze me," Cameryn had shot back. "Just let me be happy."

"Fine, fine, then happy *I* will be. Congratulations!"

So Cameryn was riding the tsunami of emotion, and she didn't care if it ever stopped. *Just ride the wave,* she told herself.

With his left hand Kyle pushed open the school door. Inside, the halls smelled of new wax. Light, streaming from high windows, caught the dust in angel beams. She saw a teacher hurry by with a black armband around her upper arm. It was too tight, and it caused the flesh to bulge.

"I should get me one of those," Kyle said softly. His face clouded with emotion as he added, "Brad Oakes was the best teacher I ever had. He taught me to write."

The Silverton High School building churned with Monday-morning activity as they made their way inside. Kids crammed the hallway, slamming lockers, hurrying before first bell.

"Hey, Scott," Kyle said, raising his chin in greeting.

"Hey, Kyle." Scott Charlton's blue eyes widened, almost imperceptibly, as he took in the fact of Cameryn. "Wow," he said, seeming to register it all. His eyes slid down past Cameryn's plain blue jeans to her scuffed boots, and then back up again to her black pea coat with the large plastic buttons. "Looks like you've had a busy weekend, Kyle."

"Yeah. You could say that," Kyle replied.

"I guess you heard about Oakes and the remembrance thing they're doing for him today. There's some assembly scheduled for first period. I'll save you a seat."

"Save two," Kyle called out as Scott hurried down the hallway.

As they walked toward the classrooms, kids moved aside. Kyle, like a boat unaware of its wake, parted them effortlessly. "I'm sorry, I didn't even ask you. Is that okay? That we go together, I mean? I'll come to your class—you've got Ward, right?"

"Yep, I start my day with biology," Cameryn replied. "And I'd really like that. I'll wait for you outside of class."

With a quick kiss on the top of her head, Kyle left her at her homeroom.

The remembrance ceremony for Mr. Oakes was exactly what Cameryn had expected it would be: girls crying unashamedly while a few boys, dry-eyed, turned red with emotion, shifting from foot to foot as they awaited their turn at the microphone. Snuffling teachers, the principal, the janitor, all streamed up to the front to say a few words while soft strains of John Denver's "Rocky Mountain High" played in the background. When the adults were finished, the students came next. Kids walked up, hesitant, afraid of the microphone, but determined to eulogize their teacher. Cameryn noticed that a few townspeople had crashed the service as well, hovering in the corner, waiting their turn. She recognized Dwayne Reynolds, his mustache drooping. He held his floppy hat in his hands. The skin on his forehead was ghostly white. She'd never seen Dwayne without the hat, and it made him look naked somehow.

Seated in a section where she hadn't sat before, Cameryn realized that from up here she could see it all.

The football team always picked the highest bleachers on the top row, which allowed them to rest their backs against the painted wall. She saw Lyric and Adam down in the second row and waved, a little sorry she wasn't with them but even more glad to be sharing the time with Kyle. Both Adam and Lyric waved back.

Dwayne Reynolds had made his way to the microphone. His voice shook as he spoke. "Brad Oakes was the finest man I ever knew. An old soul. I just wanted you kids to know that." It was all he said. After that, Dwayne walked away from the microphone and straight out a side door.

"They were really close," Kyle said softly. "They were always together." He straightened in the seat, his back pulling away from the wall. "You know what? I've got to go down there. I'm the one who found him and . . . I need to say good-bye. Do you want to?"

"Sorry, no way." Cameryn shook her head. "I'm not one for public speaking. Say good things for the both of us."

Kyle picked his way down the wooden bleachers and stood in the line, which by then had thinned out. It took only a few minutes for him to get to the mike. For some reason, Cameryn's heart was in her throat as Kyle stepped up to speak.

The crowd hushed. He cleared his throat and looked up to where Cameryn sat, and when their eyes met, he straightened. "In a world short of heroes . . ." he began. His voice sounded higher than normal, but she doubted others would notice. "Mr. Oakes was the greatest of heroes to me. He taught me to love words and to love nature. He was my Scout leader, and he showed me the beauty of our mountains and how to survive outdoors. He taught me to think, to understand both nature and life." Taking a wavering breath, he looked at Cameryn, locking onto her eyes as if he was speaking only to her. "In his class, we read F. Scott Fitzgerald. Mr. Oakes told us that Fitzgerald said, 'Show me a hero, and I'll write you a tragedy.'" Kyle's voice cracked as he finished. "Mr. Oakes, losing you is a tragedy to each and every one of us. I'll never forget you. None of us ever will."

And then, as Kyle walked away, the room did something it hadn't done for anyone else who spoke. It erupted in applause. Cameryn swelled with pride as she understood this tribute to both their teacher and to Kyle. He had said what they were all thinking, only better. Kyle had put words to what none of them could express.

Later, they all crowded in the lunchroom, where the other kids revealed what was really on their minds: they wanted to know about the death. Every gory detail.

Cameryn was sitting next to Kyle in a section dominated by the team, but this time Lyric and Adam had joined them, too. It was an odd mix but one that seemed to be working. The overarching theme was death, a canopy that encompassed them all, despite their usual habitat in different social strata.

Scott Charlton took a bite of cold pizza. "So, Cameryn," he said between chews, "you work with your dad, right? Does that mean you were at Oakes's autopsy?"

The eyes of everyone at the table suddenly turned onto her, and there was a hush. Here they were, the cheerleaders and the jocks, with their attention trained exclusively on Cameryn. She was holding a breadstick, and she felt her hand slowly drift back to her plate. She felt the full weight of the obligation. This is what they'd been waiting for, she realized: the real story. As assistant to the coroner, she was the show after the commercial break. Panic welled inside her, but Kyle put his hand firmly on her knee. He was pressing strength into her through his strong fingers.

"I was there," she admitted. "But before you ask, I can't get into it. It's still an active case."

Nodding, Scott said, "That's cool. But I heard some pretty weird stuff about the way the body looked, like . . . he didn't have any eyes." Scott held up a hand and fluttered his fingers as though they were lashes. "All I want to know is if you have any idea about what killed him?"

"Nope."

"His eyes *were* blown out, right?"

She hesitated.

"We already know. Kyle told us."

"Yes, but—"

She didn't get any further. Everyone at the table erupted with theories of what had happened to their teacher. Jessica, a thin girl with a model's face, said, "I think it's something like a rare kind of disease from South America or Africa. Since the rain forests have been cut down, all kinds of nasty stuff's gotten out."

"No," another voice protested, "he never traveled there."

"He flew, didn't he? Maybe he caught a disease on a plane."

"The last trip he took was, like, last spring. A disease wouldn't take that long to show up."

"I'm wondering if it was a ball of lightning that went right into his room."

"My dad said the sheriff put up crime-scene tape. Do you think he was murdered?"

"Who would murder Mr. Oakes? He had, like, a ton of friends. Everyone in town loved him."

"You never know."

"Wait, I have a theory, and it's a really good one," a voice said, one Cameryn finally recognized. It was Lyric. She had the floor, and she looked as though she was enjoying it. This wasn't a group that usually paid attention to her.

Lyric slid her fingers through her blue hair and then squeezed it at her crown, fluffing the locks so they fell in ringlets. Her eyes danced as she announced, "Okay. Here it is: spontaneous human combustion."

Cameryn groaned.

Lyric was sitting four people away, so she leaned forward to swivel her head toward Cameryn. "No, Cammie, I'm serious. It's a real thing. Adam and I looked it up on the Internet, and there're tons of articles about it. There've been people all over the world who, like, just"— she snapped her fingers—"burn up, right in their own beds and stuff, without any reason at all. Their houses aren't on fire or anything, not their sheets or their walls or anything around them. Go look it up if you don't believe me."

"I know all about spontaneous human combustion," Cameryn replied.

"Then you know they just find the bodies with the torso all burned up, and maybe an arm or a leg left in a pile of ash. I think maybe that's what happened to Mr. Oakes."

Cameryn tried to keep her tone even. It embarrassed her that Lyric would reveal her bizarre theories in a group like this. In Lyric's house, with her beads for curtains and her psychedelic posters covering every inch of her bedroom walls while incense wafted, Cameryn would listen to any wild hypotheses and try to give them their due. But this was different. She tried to telegraph this to Lyric, but for once her friend's psychic connection failed her. Lyric kept right on talking.

Eyes bright, Lyric began a list of the dead. "Dr. J. Irving Bentley. His body was found in the bathroom. He burned a three-foot hole though the floor, with only one section of his leg left intact on the linoleum. Everything else, even his teeth, turned to ash."

"Lyric—"

"Mary Reeser. All they found of her was backbone and a shrunken skull the size of a baseball, plus a foot in a slipper—I think it was black satin—and ten pounds of ashes. Helen Conway burned up like a Christmas log."

"All right, all right. Lyric, you've made your point. It's an interesting theory, except Mr. Oakes didn't burn up like that. He didn't turn to ash."

"You told me he was cooked."

Cameryn winced. That part wasn't supposed to get out, and she could get in real trouble if her father discovered she'd told Lyric and then Lyric, in turn, had announced it to a table of A-listers at the school. For an instant she hoped no one noticed, but then she heard the whispers buzzing as this new piece of information got passed down the table. "Cooked," she heard someone say, followed by, "No way!"

"We really don't know anything yet," Cameryn declared loudly while shooting Lyric a hard look. "That was just a theory. The autopsy results aren't in yet."

Undeterred, Lyric said, "Maybe Mr. Oakes had a *partial* spontaneous human combustion. Maybe this is something new."

"Yeah, like *that's* what happened," Kyle murmured under his breath.

Now it seemed everyone at the table was looking at Cameryn, trying to read her reaction to this latest theory. "It doesn't do any good to speculate," she argued. "Not when the results aren't in." She could feel the heat rise in her cheeks as she saw Lyric as the others must see her: a blue-haired girl with wild theories, probably believing in the Loch Ness monster and Bigfoot. Cameryn didn't want these students to think she was like that. Her interest was real science, not hokey Internet theories.

When Lyric stated, "I'm just trying to think outside the box," Cameryn forced a smile and murmured, "It's more like outside reality."

The kids at the table laughed at this, and Cameryn felt her spirits buoy. "Ooooh," Jessica cooed, "sounds like trouble in paradise."

Shocked and stung, Lyric glared at Cameryn, her eyes blue lasers. Cameryn held up her hands and said, "Sorry, Lyric, I didn't mean it to come off like that."

"Well, it did!" Adam said, speaking up for the first time. His pale skin looked even more pallid as he stood beneath the humming cafeteria lights. "Lyric put a lot of work into this idea. We were on the computer half the night, printing files. You can at least keep an open mind."

"But Adam, those people you're talking about were piles of ashes, which Mr. Oakes was not, so right there your theory doesn't fit. Besides, we know what causes spontaneous human combustion. There's something that starts it, like a dropped cigarette onto the chest of a person who has already died. The nightshirt or whatever starts to burn and the person's own fat becomes the fuel. That's not what happened here."

Indignant, Lyric grabbed her lunch and stood up beside Adam, gripping the tray so hard her fingers blanched white. "*We* know? It's bloody amazing that you always know everything about *everything*! I think Adam and I will finish our pizza somewhere else."

Cameryn was incredulous that Lyric would work herself up and overreact that way. She didn't know what to say. She could feel her own body tense as she stared, her gaze faltering, at Lyric's indignant expression. It was obvious Lyric was waiting for her to react, but Cameryn didn't know what to say with an audience looking on. She and Lyric had fought before, but never in front of witnesses. Unsure, Cameryn said nothing.

"Okay, well, have a *great* lunch," Lyric told her, glaring. Then, turning on her heel, she stomped off with Adam trailing behind.

Now Cameryn did find her voice. "No, Lyric, wait!" she cried, but Kyle, with his steadying hand, whispered, "Let her go. You guys should work this out when it's just the two of you. Cammie, I like Lyric, I really do, but . . . she seems a little intense."

"She's my best friend."

"Who probably needs a little space right now. Don't you think?"

Cameryn bit her lip as she watched Lyric's retreating figure. Adam had draped his thin arm across her, like a shawl, and Lyric's head was bent as she listened to whatever it was Adam was telling her. A moment later they were gone.

"I don't even know what happened there," Cameryn said softly. "I don't understand why she got so mad."

"She was hurt because you blew off her theory," Kyle told her. They were at the end of the lunch table, Kyle at the corner and Cameryn next to him. He pulled her toward him so that her back was now turned toward the rest of the table, and his voice was so soft she wasn't sure she understood his next words. "I think I know how she feels."

This checked Cameryn. She could feel herself wilt. "You do?"

Gently, Kyle placed his fingertip beneath her head and turned it. He moved her hair, and his lips sought her ear, touching it as lightly as a butterfly. When he whispered to her, she could feel a flush warm her skin, as though the words themselves could leave the barest imprint on her flesh. They were in the cafeteria, surrounded by a cacophony of noise, the slamming trays, the eruptions of laughter, and yet the two of them were alone in their own private, whispered space.

"Will you laugh at me if I tell you something?" Kyle asked.

"No. I'd never laugh at you."

She turned her face toward him, so close now their foreheads touched, and they held that pose for almost a minute before Kyle said, "Because, believe it or not, I have a theory, too."

His breath was hot between them.

"What is it?" she asked.

"I'm not sure I should say it out loud. Not here, anyway. Not now. I'm not sure it's even right. But it just keeps going through my head, again and again."

"I'm the assistant to the coroner. I think you should let me decide. Does it have anything to do with extraterrestrials?"

Kyle's brown eyes darkened. "I'm not kidding, Cammie."

"Sorry," she said. "Don't keep me in suspense. Lunch is almost over, and I won't be able to wait until after school. So tell me!"

Kyle took a breath and let it out slowly, a warm plume of air on her lips. For a moment he was quiet, blinking. Then he whispered, "I think . . . I think I might know who killed Brad."

Chapter Eleven

"NOW I'VE HEARD it all," her mammaw cried. "First a man dies with no explanation, and then the small-town rumors start flying like feathers in the wind. You know the story about gossip and feathers, girl?"

"Yes, Mammaw, I know the story," Cameryn replied. It was one of her grandmother's regulars, a morality tale she dragged out whenever she saw the need. Throw a handful of feathers into the wind and then try to catch them, which was impossible because the feathers had already been swept to the four corners of the earth and no one could ever gather them up again. Mammaw said the story was Irish, but Cameryn doubted this.

She couldn't help but think her mammaw's hair looked like feathers. White tufts stood out from her head, curling softly at the ends like down pulled from a pillow.

When she spoke, her soft Irish lilt curled the edges of her words, too. But Cameryn knew better than to be fooled by the soft periphery. In addition to her Irish looks, her grandmother possessed an Irish temper, and her eyes, when angry, didn't resemble the blue sky so much as cold steel.

"Don't go ignoring me when I'm telling you a truth," Mammaw said now. "You're accusing a perfectly wonderful man on no evidence at all. It's shameful, is what it is!"

Her father, who was sitting in the easy chair, looked up reluctantly from his book. "Ma," he said, "give it a rest. I think you've made your point."

"A point's not made until someone listens," Mammaw retorted.

"Why are you jumping all over Cammie? It's not her theory. She's just telling us what Kyle thinks."

"And I'm reminding you that the rambling of a young boy can do a man a lot of harm. The story should go no further than this room!"

Patrick closed the book and slowly set it down on the table beside him, beneath an imitation Tiffany lamp that had a shade made from plastic instead of glass. He'd been reading an old Louis L'Amour book, one in a series of Westerns her father called his "guilty pleasures." He pinched the bridge of his nose, and his glasses rose up on the tips of his fingers.

Cameryn sat perched on the end of the couch, elbows on knees. "Mammaw," she protested, "I'm not saying Dwayne Reynolds did anything—I'm saying it's *possible* Kyle's right about him. Maybe Dad should call the sheriff so he could check it out."

"On what basis? Because your new boyfriend has an itch?" Mammaw demanded.

Patrick sighed. "All right, all right. Let me hear the facts one more time. Cammie, tell me again, please." He took off his reading glasses and dropped them into his shirt pocket. "Slowly this time. Why does Kyle think Dwayne Reynolds is a killer?"

"Because Dwayne is the only one who had the key to Mr. Oakes's house. Remember, Dwayne gave the key to Kyle when he sent him over there. He took it off his key ring and gave it to him. You've got to admit that's a little strange."

Her father shrugged. "That's thin at best. I have a key to our neighbor's home, too, and they have ours. A key, in and of itself, does not make a person a killer."

"Of course not. But Dad, Kyle knew both men and, well, I don't want to say any more. Not now, anyway." She looked at her grandmother's face, still square and angry. There was more to the story, but Cameryn dared not tell it with her grandmother in the room.

Mammaw wore beige pants made of stretch material and a cotton top bedecked with bright tulips, far brighter than her dark expression. She seemed to realize that Cameryn was holding back. With her usual *tsk*, she picked up a doll's cloth body and its plastic head, hands, and feet, and stuffed them into a sewing bag.

Because Mammaw repaired dolls for fun and a little profit, as a child, Cameryn had often seen old dolls in various degrees of wholeness flung across her home. Arms, legs, heads, torsos—it was a joke between them that these dissected doll parts might have fueled Cameryn's desire for the real thing, building her passion for forensics. "Freud would have a heyday with you," her grandmother often quipped.

Now Mammaw was poised beneath a doorway, the doll's plastic head angled crazily from the bag drooping in her hand. "It's clear to me you want to be alone with your father," she said. "It's late and I'm going to my room to do a bit of stitching. I've got to piece this wee one together. But Cammie"—she gave Cameryn a hard look—"I can't help but notice you've placed a lot of stock in that new boyfriend of yours. Be careful where you put your heart." With that, she was gone.

"All right, now," her father said, his voice curt. "Tell me the rest of it."

She hesitated.

"I know you, Cammie. For your whole life I've watched that clever mind of yours spinning ideas. Out with it."

Cameryn straightened. The game had turned deadly

serious and she wanted to be careful how she framed the strange accusation, because she wasn't sure, even now, if there was truth in it. She remembered the words Kyle had whispered and how she'd wondered at their audacity. The bell had rung in the lunchroom, the kids had scattered, but Kyle, not caring if they were late, had pulled Cameryn into an alcove. As he spoke to her he did a curious thing: He wound her long hair around his finger until his fingertip blanched white. It didn't hurt her at all, just a gentle tugging, like a small dog feeling a leash.

"Cammie," Kyle had said at last, "I think, maybe, Brad and Dwayne were . . . more than just friends. Do you know what I'm saying?"

"You're insane."

"I saw them. I was driving on Blair Street, late. They were in the alley together."

"When?"

"About two months ago," he'd whispered. His voice had been low, quiet. "Brad was leaning his head against Dwayne, and Dwayne had his arm around him, tight. They were walking like that, and then I couldn't see them anymore."

"But . . . Dwayne's married."

Kyle's dark eyes had fluttered briefly. "As if that matters," he'd said. "A week ago something else happened. I was with Dwayne, working on a photo project at his studio and Brad just kept calling and calling Dwayne's cell. Dwayne was getting really upset. He left the room at least three times to talk to Brad. I heard him raise his voice."

"Why didn't you tell Justin this when he interviewed you at the house?" she'd demanded.

"I guess I didn't put it together, not until I saw Dwayne at the memorial just now. It's like it clicked. Maybe it's nothing," he said, and she could tell he was already doubting himself. He'd unwound her hair from his finger, and it stayed in a perfect curl. "Now that I've said it out loud, I think Lyric's theory's better. Just forget it."

"I'm not sure I can. Are you going to tell the sheriff?"

Kyle shook his head. "And get sucked into the vortex? No, I just wanted to bounce it off of you and see if you thought I was on to something. Your face is telling me everything I need to know. Look, we'd better go. We're both already late, and I don't want to lose my perfect GPA. Boy Scout, remember?"

"Kyle!"

He'd looked at her with his warm eyes.

"Don't tell what you just said to me to anyone else," she'd requested. "Not until I think about it."

The hand rose up again, only this time the fingertips grazed his forehead. "Scout's honor," he said.

All this Cameryn summed up for her father, who looked

at her, disbelieving. "So Kyle's intuition is based on some pretty weak observations," she concluded. "Should I say anything to Sheriff Jacobs, or let it pass?"

"Let me think about what I should do with this," Patrick answered, unknowingly echoing his daughter.

"Okay," she agreed, relieved to leave the responsibility behind her. But her father wasn't done with her just yet. He turned on the gas fireplace, and Cameryn heard the familiar clicking, then the gentle burst of flames as Patrick settled back and took his glasses out of his pocket. But instead of putting them on, he placed the stem of them between his teeth.

"Tell me about this boy," he said.

"Kyle? He's great. An overachiever, heading for college on the East Coast."

"He's a fast mover," her father said. "You've never been one to lose your head over a boy, Cammie. You've always been the cautious type."

"And your cautious daughter's not had a date in months. You know, I don't get it. Why is everyone so freaked out about me kissing Kyle?"

There was a beat. "You kissed?"

Cameryn's heart jumped at this slip. "That's not the point," she said. "I guess I'm surprised people aren't happier for me. Even Lyric's acting funky. I think she's jealous."

"That doesn't sound like Lyric."

Cameryn flopped back onto the couch and sighed. "You're right. She's probably just ticked because I didn't go for her wacko theory. She said Mr. Oakes burned up from partial spontaneous human combustion. When I told her it couldn't happen, she got mad and stormed off."

"Ah, that part *does* sound like Lyric. But we weren't talking about her. I was trying to talk about you and Kyle and this sudden relationship of yours. What's the rush?"

"I'm not rushing. I'm doing what every other kid in my school does. For once I'm feeling instead of thinking."

"But you've never been like all the other kids," he protested.

"Maybe I want to be."

He looked at her with genuine concern. "Why?"

Cameryn pictured her mother, pressing forward ever closer in her car, but she abruptly forced her mind away from that image. How could she explain to her father that part of Kyle's attraction was that he diverted Cameryn from her own inner life? Or that thoughts of Kyle blotted out a dreadful anticipation of the encounter that was drawing so near, whether a plague or salvation she couldn't tell. Traces of Hannah were white noise in Cameryn's soul. She knew that when she saw her mother, face-to-face, her life would change forever.

She'd tried hanging on to the beautiful lie of life with her father in their small green-shingled home. Now Kyle blotted everything out, which was exactly what Cameryn needed. But she couldn't say that out loud to her father. Instead, she shrugged and answered, "I don't know, Dad. The heart wants what it wants, when it wants it. I guess that's all there is."

When her father cleared his throat, she realized he had something more he wanted to say. His skin glowed in the fake Tiffany light, which made her wonder if he'd applied lotion to his face. That would be news. He'd always been a minimalist when it came to male primping.

"Well, you can't argue with love," he said. "I guess when it comes down to it I couldn't agree with you more."

"I never said love. I'm in 'like.'"

"Call it what you will. You know it's strange—fortuitous, really, that you should be embarking on a relationship of your own. 'The heart wants what it wants,'" he repeated her words slowly. "The thing is, something's happened in my own life that I want to talk to you about, Cammie. It seems we're on parallel tracks. Although my train is going much more slowly than yours."

Cameryn felt a rabbit kick to her ribs. "What are you talking about?"

He had on dark blue slacks with a pleat in them, and he spread his fingers over his knees. "I'm old, Cammie," he began.

"No you're not."

"Thank you for the requisite lie, but the truth is, life has a way of whipping by. When your mother reentered your life, it was like a wake-up call. It's been fourteen years since I've seen her. Fourteen years of my life, just . . . gone. I realize now how alone I've been."

"I've been here with you. And Mammaw."

"What I'm talking about is something different. I love you and Mammaw more than anything, but I want—need—a life of my own."

Of course she understood what he was saying, and her insides coiled when he said it. "Except . . . you're married," she said softly.

"In the eyes of the Church, yes. But I'm not even sure about that anymore. I've talked to Father John about filing for an annulment, and he's behind my decision. Lord knows I've got grounds." He cleared his throat, but his words still sounded strange, as though his throat had tightened. "I hope you understand."

"Are you telling me you've met someone?" she asked. It seemed best to be blunt, to lay it out there, a cold hard fact that could just be answered, yes or no. Steeling herself, she tried to prepare. She stared at her father, but he didn't meet her gaze.

"Yes. There is another woman in my life. She came when I wasn't even looking, and no one was more surprised than I was—"

With a one-word question, a bullet to pierce him as she'd been pierced, she asked, "Who?"

He waited a beat before answering. "As you may have noticed," he began, somewhat formally, "I have been spending a lot of time in Ouray." His voice softened, became his own again. "There's a judge up there that I've gotten friendly with. Friendly's not the right word. Close. Amy Green. Judge Amy Green. You'd like her, honey."

"How long?"

"A few months now."

Cameryn almost laughed at this, at the fact that they'd both been living secret lives, secret lies.

"Does Mammaw know?"

"Yes."

"Another secret between the two of you, with me left out again."

Now he did look at her, his eyes pleading for her to understand. "It wasn't like that. We thought it best to wait to see if the relationship with Amy went anywhere before I told you. Well, it has."

With a Herculean effort, she shrugged as if it didn't matter to her at all, even though she felt another plank crumbling inside. It was hard to admit, even to herself, that one of the story lines she'd imagined was that Hannah would appear at their doorstep, crying, castigating herself, and begging the two of them for mercy, and then her father would break down, too. In her mind's eye she would see him understanding Hannah's story of woe and loving her all over again. And then somehow they would become a family: father, mother, and daughter, a new trinity to replace the old. But that was the problem with fantasies. They rarely came true. And they left the one who did the imagining feeling emptier than ever, because even the dream was gone.

A word Mr. Oakes used to use played in her head like the beat of a drum: irony. Here was Hannah, poised to reenter their atmosphere, and her father had gone and found someone else. After fourteen years in limbo. The timing was nothing if not ironic.

Gently, he asked, "Do you want to know about Amy?"

Cameryn, still reeling inside, worked on hardening her inner shell. "Not particularly," she said. "I don't think I'm up for adding another woman to the equation when I haven't figured out Hannah yet."

"Understandable. Completely understandable." He looked disappointed, but he smiled to cover it. "Let's make a deal. How about if I be happy for you and Kyle, and you be happy for me and Amy?"

Cameryn forced an answering smile. "Sure. Absolutely. You know what they say—life goes on."

"If it doesn't, there's definitely something wrong." He laughed at this, but it sounded hollow. His face shifted again, and now he was earnest as he tried to explain, "Cammie, I need you to understand. Your life is just about to start and it's going to move on without me. You're a year from going out on your own and—I'm suddenly very much aware of that ticking clock."

So am I! she wanted to scream. *Hannah's on her way and I'm facing this alone and now there's no way to bring you in because now there's another woman! You've done this thing and ruined the dream.* This was the proof she needed, to confirm that their lives had pulled apart, like a braid undone. Before, there had been no secrets, and now that was all there was between them. Separate lives, lived underground. Instead of saying any of this she stared blankly at him.

"You've changed," he told her, perplexed. "I'm looking at you and I'm not seeing the same girl."

Funny, that's what Justin said when he showed me the carcass of a dog. And I'm not the same girl. I don't want to be.

"I'm not sure what to say to that, Dad. Maybe I'm growing up."

"Up is fine," he said. Then, eyes pleading, his features turned soft. "Up is fine," he said again. "Just not away."

Who knows what's coming? she argued inside. *Who can tell?*

Then, on the outside where everything counted, she answered, "Never away, Dad. I promise."

Chapter Twelve

AS CAMERYN APPROACHED the Oakes home, she heard, rather than saw, the difference. It was the silence. Rudy, Mr. Oakes's dog, had been given to a friend who lived across town, and now the backyard stood empty, with a single water dish turned on its side, giving the house an eerie feel. Trees shifted restlessly in a wind that flapped a remnant of yellow plastic tape caught on the chain-link fence, a scrap from the CRIME SCENE: DO NOT CROSS barrier.

The rest of the tape had been taken down, she knew, because the sheriff had released the crime scene the day before. "We've done everything that we know to do, and I still don't understand what in the Sam Hill I'm dealing with," Sheriff Jacobs had said. "Could be flipping aliens for all I know, and I'm not sure how to serve a warrant on green men in spaceships." Cameryn's father, handing her the balled-up yellow tape, had replied, "Something killed this man, John. And if there's a something, I bet there's a someone."

Which was what had brought Cameryn back to the Oakes house. After a lot of thought last night, Patrick had called the sheriff with Kyle's story, and Sheriff Jacobs, desperate due to the lack of clues, had decided to follow the lead. At best it was a tenuous link to a possible suspect. Following a paper-thin trail, Cameryn was here to see if that someone might be Dwayne Reynolds.

She heard a car door slam and turned to see Deputy Justin Crowley walking toward her. She hadn't noticed his car parked across the street.

"It's about time you got here," was Justin's greeting.

"Hello to you, too."

"Sorry," he said, unlocking the door. "I'm a little tense. It doesn't help that I had to wait for you to get here to even put the key in. I've been sitting in my car for almost fifteen minutes!"

He pushed open the door and stepped inside, then waved her in. But he didn't move back far enough, which meant Cameryn had to brush past him, grazing his body lightly as she entered the foyer. Justin's hair had fallen into his blue-green eyes like a wedge. Impatiently, he raked it back.

"Something you should know about me, for future reference," he said. "I hate to wait."

"I will pledge my entire life around that *incredibly*

important fact. If I ever make you wait again may I be put to death on the spot."

"I also hate sarcasm."

"Can't help you there."

Justin helped Cameryn out of her coat, hanging it on a metal hook near the door. She felt cold, and blew on her fingers to warm them.

"Before we go any further I want you to know I think this Dwayne-Brad connection is completely bogus," Justin claimed. "Rumor is not the way we're going to solve this thing. Do you have any news from the forensic front?"

"The lab work hasn't been completed yet, but nothing's changed since we were there with Dr. Moore," she told him. "Brad Oakes fried in his own bed. Manner of death—unknown. So far, no one has a clue, so we're pretty much grasping at straws."

"The difference is, these straws can destroy innocent people." A beat later, he added, "I talked to Dwayne today."

"And?"

"And . . . he said he knew Brad fairly well, but he had the key to the house just in case he needed to get Scouting equipment at the last minute. He also said they didn't socialize much beyond Boy Scouts. For what it's worth, I believe him."

"We'll have to see. And by the way," Cameryn mentioned, pulling a pair of latex gloves from her bag, "you could have started without me."

"No, I couldn't. The law, remember?"

She wiggled her fingers into the end of the gloves. "Ah, yes, I remember. Colorado State Statute 30-10-606. Having a coroner present allows you to recheck a formerly released scene without going through the hassle of securing a new search warrant. As long as I'm here you can step oh-so-neatly around the law. Am I right?" She watched Justin's face as it registered surprise, his dark brows arcing into his hairline.

There was another pause. "How old are you again?"

"Seventeen. Eighteen in January."

He blew out a breath, like steam escaping from a kettle. "Hard to believe," he said. "You are the oldest kid I've ever met."

Justin's badge was actually pinned on his shirt this time, but his jeans looked as though he'd been riding a motorcycle. There were grass smudges, dirt. The hem of his pants was encrusted with mud. Cameryn, at least, was clean. She had on jeans, faded but just washed, and her favorite sweater. The sleeves were too long, which meant she was forever pushing them up to free her hands, but the fabric made it worth the hassle. Chenille yarn, soft as velvet, in a Dublin-green color made her think of moss on stone.

"How'd you get so dirty?" she asked him.

"I went looking for the dog carcass I dumped down the mountain."

This surprised her. "Really? I wanted to look, too. I know the sheriff says there's no connection, but I thought it should be checked. Did you find it?"

"Nope. Body's already scavenged and gone. Not a trace left, at least that I could see. But at this point I want to follow every thread I can because nothing about this case makes sense. So far we've got a dead man and zero evidence." He held up his hand, ticking off his fingers one by one. "We got no motive. We got no weapon. Brad had no enemies and there's no money trail. We got blown-out eyeballs and cooked flesh and a crime scene that's completely clean. I don't know what happened in this house. We may be looking at the perfect crime."

The thought chilled her enough that she didn't speak. In that slice of silence she could hear the wind outside howl mournfully, the harbinger of a coming storm. This was the time of year when Silverton itself became frozen in a layer of snow. The townspeople still existed, of course, but they were like fish in a winter pond, alive beneath the glassy ice but living in an ever-shrinking sphere. If there was evidence outside, it was about to get buried until spring. But forensics looked *inside*, into the very corpuscles themselves, if necessary, to let a body tell its own story.

To be here, she'd had to miss another shift at the

Grand, which worried her a little. If she missed too many shifts she might lose that job. It didn't pay a lot but it was steady, or at least it had been until she became so involved in what she was doing as assistant to the coroner. She was thinking about this when Justin said, "Sheriff Jacobs is up in Ouray, filing for a search warrant to let us get the phone records legally. Your presence here is just to jump-start the process until we get the right papers."

"I know. My dad's with him."

Justin cocked his head. "Why'd Pat go?"

"Because my dad's hoping to obtain a search warrant issued through Judge Amy Green. He's got a . . . connection . . . with her. He thinks she'll write it if he's the one doing the asking." Cameryn felt a pang when she said this, but Justin didn't seem to notice. He was already on his knees, intent on a stack of DVDs.

"Wow," Justin said. He held up several jewel-boxed DVDs toward the light, squinting at the titles. "Here's some disturbing news. Looks like our Mr. Oakes was a wild one."

"Is that porn?"

"*National Geographic* special on the life of Tolkien, *The Lord of the Rings* complete DVD set, and *Shakespeare in Love*. Here's another one that's pretty extreme—*Emma*. Wasn't that a chick flick? Hmmmm, maybe Kyle's on to something after all."

"Not funny." Cameryn drummed her fingers on the desktop. "While you're investigating his movie selection, what exactly am I supposed to be doing?"

"Try to find any evidence of a too-close relationship with Dwayne. We weren't looking for that before. Cards, pictures, phone records—if you see anything, just bring it to me."

"Exactly when did I become your page?" she asked tartly.

"I think this comes under the Justin-could-use-the-help heading."

"I'm assistant to the coroner, not a detective."

"Pretend the house is a body and you'll do fine."

It felt wrong, searching through Brad Oakes's things. Although Statute 30-10-606 was on the books, it was supposed to be invoked only when a coroner wanted to try and match a murder object to a wound. Justin, though, was skating through the legal loophole, which meant if this search ever went to court they were on very thin ice. Her eyes skimmed only the surfaces while Justin pulled out drawers and carefully rifled through the contents.

The house was bare, spartan, its major decoration being several bookshelves that stretched the length of the entire living-room wall. She walked past them slowly, her gloved fingertips stroking the spines, each one by a famous author and all hardbound. Dostoyevsky,

Fitzgerald, René Descartes, C. S. Lewis—she felt she did not belong here, prying through her teacher's mind. She'd already been through his body, and that should have been enough.

"We're not going to find anything, you know," Justin called out. He opened the bottom cabinet of a china hutch and pulled out a large amber bottle, round at the bottom with a golden foil lid. "Oakes had good taste in booze. This is Chivas Regal, sixty bucks a bottle. And it's unopened. Did I tell you I think Kyle O'Neil's sent us on a fishing expedition?"

"Why would he do that?" Cameryn picked up an Indian pot that was encircled at the base in a brick-red pattern. She looked inside. It was empty.

"I don't know. It's a vibe of his. I think he gets off on power."

She was about to set down the pot, but her hand stopped midair. "What do you mean?"

"I mean one accusation from Kyle and everyone has to start jumping through hoops. Search warrants. Interviews. I get the feeling he's sitting back, enjoying this."

"He was *trying* to help," Cameryn said, bristling. "I was the one he talked to. Kyle wasn't even sure we should say anything! You're not being fair. You don't even know him."

"Hey, pull in the claws. You're right, I don't know the

guy, just the type." He shifted his gaze around the room. "I'm not finding anything. How about you?"

She started to shake her head, but then she did see something, although it had nothing to do with Dwayne. On a shelf was a plain picture frame, and the face inside it was a woman's. The features were soft, but her smile was anything but. It lit the face from within, crinkling the skin beneath her eyes and dimpling her cheeks. Her hair was warm brown.

"Did Mr. Oakes have any next of kin?" Cameryn asked.

"One sister in Florida is all we could discover, and she apparently died about two months ago. Car crash."

Sister. It must have been the woman in the picture. Cameryn could see the resemblance now, the shadow of her teacher in the smiling face. "So who inherits if there's no relative?"

"Oakes just changed his will. It all goes to the Boy Scouts of America. But before you go thinking of a motive, Brad Oakes's net worth is less than twenty thousand dollars, and that's including the fair market value of this house minus the mortgage still due, if and when the house sells. Hardly enough to kill for."

"People have murdered for less."

"Not if they have to pay a realtor. Try hitting the bedroom to see what, if anything, turns up. I'll go through the kitchen."

She made her way to the bedroom, moving carefully, trying to disturb things as little as possible. The bed was stripped and empty, sadly impersonal. Everything had already been taken from it, leaving no evidence, so she went to the dresser instead.

On its top she saw a stack of photos of Brad rappelling down a mountain—whoever had snapped the pictures wasn't in any of them. There was another book of poetry, this one by Keats. Feeling like a voyeur, she pulled open drawers, flipped through magazines, took out his empty shoes. Nothing that she could see suggested anything more than a man who loved literature and the outdoors. She turned to leave, giving the room one last glance.

It was the flowers, the ones on the nightstand, that caught her eye. When she'd been there the first time they'd been dry, like moth's wings, but now they had undergone another metamorphosis. Cameryn walked to the flowers and stared, because they weren't flowers anymore. Only the withered stalks remained, curving in a glass. The petals themselves had crumbled to dust. Yellow, lavender, and blue powdered the top of the night-stand, mingling in a sorbet of color. There was no scent. Puzzled, she'd just put her finger into the residue when she heard Justin cry out, "Oh, man! Cammie, you got to get in here. Hurry—I'm in his office."

Wiping her fingertip on her jeans, she raced to the office. When she rounded the corner, she saw Justin sitting in the rolling chair behind the desk. In his hand was a thick document, stapled at the top. He didn't look up.

"What is it?" Cameryn asked.

Justin pointed to the papers, smoothing them until they lay flat. "This is Brad Oakes's cell-phone bill from last month. Take a look."

Leaning over his shoulder, Cameryn tried to make sense of the figures. Almost instantly her eyes registered the fact that one phone number, almost exclusively, filled the blue and white lines. Day after day, night after night, it repeated itself again and again, like a phone book with only one listing. 555–3813; 555–3813; 555–3813. It marched down the page, connecting two people, a link of indisputable evidence.

"I'm assuming this number belongs to Dwayne Reynolds," she said.

"Bingo."

A sinking feeling spread through her gut, because even though it had been Kyle who suggested the possibility, she hadn't wanted to believe it.

"He told me they didn't talk much," Justin said. "He told me it was just about Scouting. Who talks about merit badges at three in the morning?"

"There might be a reason."

"If there was a *reason*, Dwayne wouldn't have lied to me. I'm looking at proof, black and white, that he's hiding something. Where there's smoke, there's fire."

"What about his wife? She must have known something about these calls."

"They've been separated since June. Dwayne's alone."

"Oh."

A low tide bogged her down as she saw the evidence pointing to a secret life. This wasn't about a lifestyle—it was about lying and deceit and other people who got hurt when they stood in the way. Dwayne's wife, his child— they might be the victims who'd been caught in a vortex of a double life. Or maybe they'd stumbled upon a truth and Dwayne couldn't find the way out.

"You're shaking, Cammie," Justin told her.

Cameryn commanded herself to stop, and she did.

Justin rubbed the back of his neck. "It's not a smoking gun, but get a load of the weird times. Two thirty-seven A.M. Four oh-five A.M. Here's one, right on the stroke of midnight. These go on right up until Brad died. Why would he make phone calls in the middle of the night?"

"Could it have anything to do with drugs? Buying, selling, that kind of thing?" Even when Cameryn asked it, she knew it couldn't be true. Her teacher had always told the class that they should alter their minds with ideas, nothing else. "Staying sober is the way to keep your mind clear and ready to think," he'd said, more than once. "Never numb yourself to life."

"It's possible," Justin said, "that they were into some

sort of scheme, but I doubt it. We didn't find any kind of drugs on our first search. Not so much as a marijuana leaf. And you'd think Oakes'sd have more money in his account if he were doing that kind of stuff."

Nodding, Cameryn added, "There's another thing that doesn't make sense. Supposing Dwayne did it. Just for the sake of argument. We still don't have any idea of *how*."

"There's a lot of chemicals used in photography, and he's a photographer."

"No chemicals that will burn a person from the inside out."

"You got anything better?"

"At this point, no," she admitted.

"So we're back to the possibility of a secret relationship. If Oakes was having some sort of a meltdown, if Dwayne was scared the secret was about to get out, well, that could supply a motive to 'off' Oakes."

Cameryn didn't answer this. Instead, she remembered seeing Dwayne in his floppy hat, teaching his son to fly-fish in the Animas River. She asked, "What happens now?"

"We found one set of prints in the bedroom that we couldn't identify. It didn't match anything in the database and it wasn't Kyle's. Now we've got enough to get a ten-print card off of Dwayne and check his prints against what we found on the nightstand and headboard. If it's a match . . ." He didn't finish, and Cameryn didn't make him.

Straightening, she looked at her watch. "The funeral's in forty minutes and I need to go. I don't want to be late. Besides, you got what you came for."

"It's a start. We'll have a much more intensive search when the court order shows up."

She signed the supplemental indicia evidence form, noting the date and time she'd arrived, then picked up the phone records.

"I'll get you a copy of these tomorrow," she told him. "I can't do it now because of the funeral."

"This whole thing with you being assistant to the coroner is still mind-bending, Cammie. I mean, you, not me, get to take this evidence with you. In effect, I'm answering to you. Weird."

"I've been deputized, Deputy. I'll try not to abuse my power. And I've got to get out of here or my mammaw will have a hissy fit. I'm driving her to the funeral."

Before she could go, she felt Justin's hand envelop hers. It was warm, and there were calluses on his palm. His skin was dry and rough. He kept his hand over hers, and that fact alone made her breath catch in her throat.

"Cammie," he said. His look was intense enough that she could feel the atmosphere vibrate like hummingbird wings. "Cammie," he said her name again, and this time his voice dropped low. "I know this isn't the right time, but it seems there really never is a right time, you know? I need to talk to you."

"What are you doing, Justin?"

"Don't look so panicked—I just want to talk. Words, that's all."

Her heart beat harder, and even though she willed it, she couldn't quiet its sound. She stared into Justin's blue-green eyes and saw more than she'd seen there before. A new emotion moved like a current underwater.

"I wanted to tell you—" He shook his head. "No, I had this all worked out, but now I can't remember how to say it."

And then Cameryn thought, *Don't do this, Justin. If you wanted to start something you should have done it before Kyle, but not now, because this is how the lies begin and I can't go there.* She knew the way that tiny seeds of deception planted into souls could sprout, intertwining one to another, and she was with Kyle now. She had no business letting Justin Crowley hold on to her hand, no business talking with him like this. Or liking it.

"I've got a funeral to go to." Gently, she pulled her hand free.

He stared at her, perplexed. "I didn't say what I wanted to say."

For a moment she didn't speak. As she stood next to a dead man's desk, she didn't feel time moving. Everything within her was as frozen as without.

"I've got a funeral to go to," she said again. "Justin, I need to leave. Do you understand?"

Outside, the winds kicked up harder, shaking the branches across the windowpanes, rattling them. She reached the door to the office but stopped when she heard his words behind her, soft and sad.

"You've changed," he said. "I told you that before, but I didn't realize how much you have. You're different. "

Cameryn was almost out the door when she turned to him. Wrapped in the protective folds of her moss-green sweater, she said, "I am. And I'll never be the same again."

Chapter Thirteen

PEALS FROM THE organ poured out of the back of St. Patrick's Catholic Church in a melodious waterfall, greeting the mourners with an ancient, medieval sound Cameryn had known since childhood. As she made her way down the aisle, she had to admit she was surprised to see so many people crammed into the pews. Townsfolk sat shoulder to shoulder, their coats beading water from the melted snow, their hair dotted with snowflakes that had transformed into crystal droplets. If Mr. Oakes could see them from heaven, Cameryn thought, he would be happy with the turnout.

"Over there," her mammaw said, pointing to a space in the back corner, directly beneath the stained-glass window depicting Jesus cradling a lamb. The lights on the inside, though, made the picture almost impossible to see. If she hadn't known what it looked like in the daylight, it would have been difficult to tell.

"Grab it before someone else sits down. Another minute and the church will be standing room only."

They settled into the wooden pew, and Cameryn studied the program printed with a picture of a lily on the front. Beneath it, in fluid script, were the words: *In Loving Memory.* After she'd read the name beneath, her eyes drifted to the front of the church, and she received a shock. In front of the altar stood a small table, draped in a lacy cloth. On either side of the table were dozens of flower arrangements in every color and shape imaginable. But on the table, and in the midst of the forest of blooms, sat a plain marble urn the color of teakwood. A picture of Mr. Oakes, smiling, was off to one side.

"Brad Oakes was *cremated*?" she whispered. "I thought the Church didn't allow that."

"Shush," her mammaw said. "That was changed in the late nineties. The Vatican doesn't like it, but it's permitted under special circumstances."

Cameryn tried not to think of her teacher's body, flayed open on the autopsy table, revealing the gray-red color of his flesh. That was one of the hardest parts of the job she did, she decided. It was knowing what really went on in the business of death. Death wasn't like sleep. It was a bloody mess.

"Oh, I hope Father John's prepared a good eulogy,"

Mammaw murmured as she unwound a scarf from her head. "He's got a full house."

"The whole town's here," Cameryn agreed. "I've never seen so many flowers."

"It's not a wonder. Brad Oakes was a great man, and his friendships ran deep. My friend Marion—you know her, she works in the rectory—told me Dwayne Reynolds put this whole funeral together—the program, the cremation, everything—and he's not even Catholic." She made the usual *tsk*ing sound between her teeth. "And it's a pity your father couldn't get back in time, but the snow's making it awfully slow between Ouray and here. Is that Lyric in the back there?"

At the sound of the name, Cameryn felt her scalp jump. Craning her neck, she saw Lyric standing by the door, her blue hair flecked with snow. It was the first time Cameryn had seen Lyric not wearing a bright color. A black coat hung loose to the floor, and beneath it she wore what Cameryn guessed was one of her mother's dresses, a shapeless dark sack that reached to the tops of her Mayura biker boots. For an instant it was like seeing someone, for the first time, in a black-and-white photo—it altered Lyric somehow. Cameryn watched her brush the snow off her coat and eye the crowd. When she saw Cameryn, she looked away.

"I'm sorry, Mammaw," Cameryn said, "but I've got to go talk to her. Save my seat."

"Don't be too long, girl! It's about to start!"

Just as they thought, St. Patrick's had filled up. Now people were standing in the foyer, two deep, and tiny puddles were forming beneath their shoes. Lyric might have moved away from Cameryn under normal circumstances, but now she had no way to get past the sea of people pressing to come in.

"Hi," Cameryn said.

"Hi." Lyric's eyes shifted away. "Where's your boyfriend?"

"I don't know. He should have been here by now. Where's yours?"

"Working at the Grand."

"Do you want to sit with Mammaw and me?"

"There's, like, twelve inches of pew there," Lyric answered. "I doubt I'd fit."

"You could try."

"What'll happen when Kyle shows up? You gonna put me on the floor?"

Cameryn compressed her lips. "I wouldn't do that."

"Excuse me," said a young woman holding a toddler. Lyric moved back to let the woman squeeze by. The foyer, jammed with damp bodies, smelled like old wood.

"You wouldn't do that," Lyric resumed. "Just like you wouldn't burn me in front of everyone in the cafeteria."

"Come on, you're overreacting."

"Please don't say that. I *hate* it when you say that."

"Which is, in itself, an overreaction. Sorry," Cameryn said as Lyric glared at her. "What I was trying to do at the lunch table was pull the conversation back to some sphere of reality. You were going on and on about spontaneous human combustion—"

"—which happens to be a *real* and true phenomenon—"

"—that has *nothing* to do with this case!"

"How do you know?"

Lyric's voice rose, and Cameryn was suddenly aware that people were staring at them. An elderly lady with a peacock hat put her finger to her lips and shook her head. As she did, the feathers trembled.

But Lyric didn't seem to care. "You're not infallible, Cammie," she said, glaring. "You just think you are."

"Ladies!" interrupted a wobbly voice. "This is a funeral. If you two want to talk, why don't you go outside for a moment until you get it all settled." It was Gus, an ancient man who ushered at St. Patrick's. Stooped almost in half, his white head dipping as he spoke, he pointed to the door leading out into the storm. "Go on, girls."

"I guess he wants us to take it outside," said Cameryn.

"Guess so." Lyric jerked her coat tight, and Cameryn, who still wore hers, opened the wooden door, neatly stepping sideways to avoid a family on their way inside. The two of them hurried down the stairs and rounded the corner where a cluster of trees stood, offering them some shelter and, more importantly, privacy. The wind whirled fat snowflakes as big as dandelion fluff.

For a moment Cameryn didn't know what to say. One thing was for sure—the cold and snow would go a long way to make them settle things quickly. "That's the first time I've ever been thrown out of a church," she said. "If Mammaw finds out I'll have to do some serious penance. Maybe bake something."

Shrugging, Lyric kept her eyes on her boots. They had silver studs on them, like tiny quills.

"Look, I'm sorry," Cameryn told her. "I came off like a know-it-all in the cafeteria. That's not what I meant to do."

Still clutching her coat beneath her chin, Lyric raised her eyes, saying, "That's not it."

"Then what's going on?"

"It's you. You're . . . different." She paused. "You're saying stuff and doing things you never used to do."

Cameryn bit her lip. This again. "I'm different because things *are* different," she replied. "You know what I'm going through."

"No, it's more than that."

Cameryn sighed. "All right. Maybe I'm just trying to keep my head straight until I see Hannah."

"But your head's *not* straight. As your best friend I'm going to tell you I know what's screwing with your mind. It's Hannah, Cammie. That's where it all started."

"We need to get inside," Cameryn muttered. "We can

talk about this later." She tucked her hands beneath her armpits. Cold was bleeding into her, but Lyric stood rooted on the spot.

"See, that's what you do, Cammie. Change the subject, leave, whatever it takes. Just *talk to me*. Right now. I deserve it. I've helped you, covered for you, listened to you make your plans. I'm your best friend, Cammie." She was pleading now. "You can't see it, but the secrets are poisoning you."

"That's not true."

Lyric's eyes went wide. Those pale blue eyes, ringed in black, now seemed to overwhelm her face. "This thing's eating you up, this lying to your family. I don't get it. Why won't you just tell them that Hannah's coming?"

"I can't!"

"Why not?"

Cameryn didn't know how to answer, so she said nothing. A car drove by, kicking up slush as it rounded the corner, then disappeared, and she wanted more than anything to be in that car, driving away.

The stained-glass windows glowed with bright color. Lit from within, their pattern could now be seen from outside the brick church. But she knew that once she reentered the sanctuary, that same light would make the glass so dark it would appear almost black. And then she had a strange thought: Was she like those windows? Maybe the only ones who could really see her stood outside, at least when the world was dark. She wondered at this. Inside her head, her life made sense, but outside . . . Could Lyric be right?

In a soft voice, barely above a whisper, Cameryn said, "I'm lying to my family because they lied to me first."

Lyric took a step closer to answer, "No, Cammie. They just didn't tell you about Jayne. That's not the same."

"There's more than you know. My dad's seeing another woman. A judge in Ouray."

"That's still not lying."

"In the eyes of the Church it is. They're still married, Lyric. My mom and my dad never got a divorce."

"They haven't seen each other in forever!" Lyric cried. "What do you expect is going to happen? You're blowing smoke, Cammie. What did Hannah say to you when she called?"

"Other . . . things," she finally confessed. "She said my dad didn't tell me the truth, that what he told me about her was all wrong. She said I shouldn't believe everything I've been told because I don't know the real story. I want to hear what Hannah has to say, and then I'll decide. What if she's right? What if everything I've believed about my life is a lie?"

"Oh, Cammie," Lyric answered softly. "I wish you'd told me before." Lyric shook her head while the snow danced around her. The tip of her nose was turning red, but her heavy, chunky, black boots had to be keeping her feet warm. Cameryn wore a velvet skirt and dress shoes, but unlike that time in the cemetery with Kyle, she wasn't numb. She could feel everything.

Through the vibrating window, the organ throbbed out the overture to Mozart's requiem, signaling the beginning of Mass. Cameryn looked up. "It's starting. We'd better get inside."

"You're all messed up, Cammie. I know you'll be mad but I've got to say it. Why would you believe a stranger over your own father? It's insanity."

Cameryn's heart constricted. "You're my best friend. Can't you even try to understand?"

"You can't turn your back on your life."

She felt her face go rigid, her fists ball up tight. She'd let someone inside her, and it had backfired. Lyric didn't . . . couldn't . . . understand. It was a mistake, telling her. Cameryn should have stuck with her plan and handled it alone.

"You know what, Lyric? We're done," she said. There was a space between every word. "I'm going in. My teacher's dead."

She didn't wait for Lyric to respond. Half-running, Cameryn turned and left the shelter of the trees. Moments later she leaped up the stairs and hurried inside the church.

It was warm inside, the air almost stifling as she took a deep breath. With the palms of her hands she rubbed her cheeks, wiping away any trace of tears or melted snow, then ran the back of her hand beneath her nose. No one noticed her because they were all watching the show up front.

"Cammie, are you all right?"

It was Kyle. Kyle, who could tell in an instant that something was wrong. "What is it?"

Fearing she might cry, Cameryn looked away.

"Come on."

While Father John's voice intoned a prayer, Kyle took her hands and led her to the back staircase, the steps that rose to the choir loft, the one place in the church that was still empty. Quietly, quickly, he drew her up the narrow stairs until they were halfway in between the loft and the church, a kind of Purgatory of its own. He sat down and pulled her next to him, and when she looked down she saw her own oxblood skirt hiding her feet.

She knew the organist wouldn't be down until the funeral was over, which meant she was safe here. If Lyric came into the church, she wouldn't be able to see Cameryn. No one could.

"The funeral's too much for you, isn't it?" Kyle asked.

"I'm just tired."

She could hear Dwayne Reynolds speaking into the microphone at the front of the church, reading a quote for Mr. Oakes.

"*. . . for this is a journey of unknowables—of unan-*

swered questions, enigmas, incomprehensibles, and most of all, things unfair," he read. "Madame Jeanne Guyon wrote these words when her own world made no sense. . . ."

For a moment Cameryn thought she couldn't breathe. The candles, blinking beneath the Christ child, seemed to have sucked up the oxygen. Maybe there were too many people exhaling carbon dioxide. Or maybe it was Kyle himself. She felt lightheaded, dizzy.

His large hazel eyes bored into hers. "I can help if you'll let me," he whispered.

"That's just it. No one can help me."

"I can. I think you're an angel."

"Angel of Death," she croaked. "That's what they call me. Whatever I touch dies."

His lips curled softly. "I'm here. And I'm alive."

She looked at him, comforted, because that was true. "Can you take me out of this place?"

He traced the pad of his finger beneath her eye, lightly wiping away a new tear.

"Let's just drive somewhere. Please?"

"In this storm?" He pulled her head to his shoulder, and for a second she forgot the pounding of her temples. "Why don't you tell me what's going on," he invited.

Because it was almost dark in the staircase, and because she couldn't see his face and in many ways he was still a stranger, a door inside her sprang open. Lyric had judged her. Her father and her mammaw would never understand. But Kyle was a clean slate, without preconceived ideas of who she had become. How could he accuse her of changing if he hadn't known who she'd been before? He was perfect, like a white sheet of paper, or untrod snow.

She took a deep, wavering breath, then closed her eyes and began, "I want to tell you about my mother. . . ."

Chapter Fourteen

THE BAR AT the Grand was made of heavy mahogany, and behind it stood a mirror that spanned the length of the wall. Above the mirror were three carved arches, the middle one larger, the side arches smaller, like a triptych, Cameryn thought. She wiped down the surface of the bar, and as she did so she caught a glimpse of her face in the mirror. What she saw surprised her: The girl with the hollowed cheeks and large, dark eyes was smiling. Actually smiling.

It still amazed her. Three days had passed since the funeral, and there was a grin on her face. She had a paper due on Monday and still she beamed. Because when she was with Kyle, she was full up, as though she were a helium balloon that couldn't hold another blast from the canister or she would pop. After being empty for so long, it felt marvelous.

That night, in the stairwell of the church, she had told Kyle everything, and he had understood her, promised to help her, said that he was there for her. Never before had she been able to share so much of her life so freely. He asked about her mammaw and her father and what she knew about Hannah, then surprised her by telling her she'd done the exact right thing. "Some problems have to be sorted out in your own mind before you let anyone else tell you what to think. You were smart to keep things quiet," he'd told her. "Wait and see what she's like before you go and blow your world apart."

Kyle even wanted to know everything about forensics, which thrilled her, too. He wasn't appalled or squeamish at the fact that her hands had been inside Mr. Oakes, or over the truth that she had held her teacher's heart and weighed his liver on a stainless steel scale. When she'd told him that, he'd traced his finger across her palm, saying, "It's sort of mystical. It's like, when you held his brain, you held Brad's thoughts in your hands."

Then came the biggest surprise of all. He'd said, "I'm rethinking my plans for college. Maybe I should go into forensics with you." Once again she noticed the flecks in his eyes, shimmering like bits of light. "Can you imagine what two forensic pathologists would be like together? You and me, Cammie. A forensic team. We'd rock."

It was the word "together" that had her humming. Now, as she cleaned the Grand, she let it roll on her tongue while she repeated it softly. "Together," she whispered aloud. And as she did, she looked at the picture of the voluptuous, turn-of-the-century woman hanging over the antique player piano. Pausing, she studied the face, with its sly grin. *You're thinking of someone, too, aren't you?* Cameryn mused. The woman, with her enormous thighs, round belly, and hint of a double chin beneath a heart-shaped face, was beautiful. Reclining on a bed of grass, one arm lifted to the sky, the woman seemed to be reaching for something just beyond her fingertips. Cameryn thought she understood this because she, too, had been reaching. But unlike the woman in the painting, she had grasped her prize.

Cameryn turned to the microwave behind the bar and began to scrub this, too. Her boss had warmed a cheese sauce, which had exploded, leaving a confetti pattern of cheddar inside. As she wiped it away, her thoughts turned to Lyric. Guiltily, she had chosen not to deal with the strain that began the night of the funeral. Or rather, Lyric had chosen. Lyric hadn't called, and Cameryn, taking the cue that her friend was still upset, decided to let things cool off before pressing. Besides, all her energy had been redirected to Kyle. Everything else was a distraction.

Out of the coroner of her eye she saw a shadow pass the Grand's window. *Don't come in here!* she thought. In ten more minutes she would be off her shift. The front section was empty, and there were only two families and a gaggle of old-timers in the back, ticketed and ready to go. Monica was already in the kitchen, preparing to take over, chatting with the Ukrainian cook while she waited. Cameryn hated to start a new table at the end of a shift. But sure enough, at that moment the bell on the door jingled, and she looked up to see not a customer but Justin, this time in Timberline boots and a blue flannel shirt. He carried a large manila folder in his hand.

"I've got news," he said, waving the envelope through the air. "The fingerprints came back." He walked to the bar but stopped, squinting at her. "You look different."

Cameryn sighed as she folded her dishcloth. "Don't start, Justin."

"No, I meant it in a good way. You look . . . happy. Uncharacteristically happy."

"Well," she said, "I am."

"Really."

Justin raked back his hair, exposing a forehead that was almost a shade lighter than his cheeks. His feet had been planted far apart; she thought he looked more like a lumberjack than a deputy. "Is it because you're with Kyle O'Neil?" he asked.

Not knowing what to say, she began to scrub the bar with her towel, the same section she had already wiped down. Finally, she answered, "News travels fast."

"Then it's true?"

More scrubbing. "Uh-huh."

She raised her eyes. Justin's brow had furrowed, and his lips had pressed thin.

"So when we were in Oakes's home and I was trying to talk to you about . . ." The words seemed to die in his throat. "Was he the reason?"

Hesitant, she nodded. "Kyle and I—we have a lot in common," Cameryn answered, folding the towel into a smaller and smaller square. She was not liking this conversation.

Justin stood rooted, not saying a word.

She tried again. "Kyle's—he's in my grade at school. We're both seniors."

Walking the last few feet, Justin didn't stop until he was directly in front of her, his green-blue eyes intense. Cameryn had stopped folding the cloth because the square was as small as it could go. Her hand clutching the rag was completely still, as though the power from her arm had been shut off. She swallowed, realizing her mouth was very dry.

"Justin," she began, "you and me—you know we're better off as friends. We work together and things could get . . . the thing is, you can never have too many friends. Right?"

A beat, and then, "Right."

She waited for him to say something more. He didn't. "So if you think I'm right then why are you glaring at me?"

"I'm not glaring. I'm thinking."

"About what?"

"I don't know. Maybe that a true friend would ask you some hard questions. Like, what are you doing with this guy, Cammie? What do you really know about him?"

The good feeling inside her vanished like water into sand. "I know enough," she snapped.

"Maybe. But you go from zero to a hundred with him in no time flat, and that's not like you. Think back to when I asked you about Kyle the day we found Oakes's body. You told me Kyle was a player."

"No I didn't! I did *not* say the word 'player.' I would never have said that about Kyle! And how can you know what's 'like me' or what isn't 'like me'? You didn't even know me before you moved to Silverton and how long has that been? Four months? What I do and who I do it with is none of your business!"

Stung, Justin turned away and lowered his head. For a moment it looked as though he was about to say something but then, apparently thinking better of it, he shook his head. "You know what?" he said. "You're right. What you do is none of my business."

Cameryn took a step back, unsure how to deal with this reversal. "I'm sorry, Justin. I didn't mean all that. It's just—"

"No, no, no, you're right. About all of it. Sometimes I forget how new I am in this town. Anyway"—he let out a breath—"we should talk about the case. That's actually the reason I came here."

"What's going on?"

"I've got some new information." He glanced around the Grand. "Is now a good time, or do you want me to come back later?"

"No. Now is good." She was uncomfortable with the intensity of his eyes, so she covered up by launching into motion. "But first, let me get you a Coke," she said. "Or do you want something else?"

"Coke's fine."

While Justin slid onto a barstool, she poured two fountain drinks into glasses usually reserved for beer and set one in front of him. The foam bubbled up into a thick head but stopped just short of spilling over. She took a sip from her own glass and tried to pretend the conversation hadn't happened. That was all they could do, really, as far as Cameryn was concerned. Act as if things were the same as before. Send it all underground.

"So," she said, her voice artificially bright, "did you find out about the fingerprints?" She pointed to the folder with her glass. "Was it a match?"

Justin shifted gears, his internal movement mirrored on his face. His expression became more serious, as if he was suddenly aware of the families chatting twenty feet away. Leaning forward on his elbows, his hands high, he dropped the manila folder onto the polished wood.

"It's a match," he said softly. "Dwayne was in that bedroom. Prints were all over the headboard. They were on the nightstand and the dresser, too—all Dwayne's."

It took two seconds for Cameryn to process this. "So Kyle was right. They had a secret relationship."

"That's what the evidence seems to suggest," Justin agreed. "But I think Kyle got the reason wrong. We all got it wrong."

"I don't understand. You have the phone calls, the prints, plus the fact he lied to you."

"Dwayne wasn't lying, exactly. He couldn't admit what was really going on because of the rules of confidentiality."

"What do you mean? Last I checked, Dwayne was not a priest."

Justin lowered his voice and leaned in even closer. "What I'm going to say next is for your ears only. I'm only telling you because you're part of the case."

At that moment, Monica hurried by. "You can leave now, Cammie!" she called out cheerily. "You want me to clock you out?"

"Sure. Thanks!" Cameryn replied. When Monica left, Cameryn leaned closer. "I know better than to spill anything, Justin." They were no more than four inches apart, so near his breath mingled with hers, heating the air between them. "What is it?" she whispered.

"Dwayne's a member of Alcoholics Anonymous. So

was Brad. They were in the organization together. They attended meetings up in Montrose so no one in Silverton would know. Dwayne was Brad's sponsor."

"His sponsor?"

"Dwayne didn't want to tell me any of this the first time I interviewed him because of A.A.'s strict rules of privacy. They really live by a code."

"Are you *serious*?" It took a moment for Cameryn to take it in. "Mr. Oakes was an alcoholic?" She pictured her teacher, perched on the edge of his desk, seeming to be without a care. He'd always been upbeat—joyful, really—as he shared his love of literature. Mr. Oakes told them the printed words were like fireflies, and if they could catch enough of them they'd light up their own worlds, and when he told them this great truth his eyes would light up, too. This was a man who so effectively hid his pain, whatever it might have been, that no one had caught on. The real secret, it seemed, was hidden in his life.

"That is so incredibly sad," she finally said. "I had him for English and saw him every day in school, and I would never have guessed."

"I went with Jacobs yesterday to interview Dwayne, and I told him about the match on the fingerprints. When Dwayne realized how serious it looked, he changed his tune and started talking. It turns out that Brad Oakes was an alcoholic who fell off the wagon when he found out his only sister died—his only living relative, killed in a car crash. *That's* what Kyle saw in the alley that night. He saw Brad drunk."

"So when Brad had his head on Dwayne's shoulder—"

"Dwayne was trying to get him home. He carried Brad to his house and put him to bed, which explains the fingerprints."

"And you can't tell how old a fingerprint is—"

"Exactly. A year-old fingerprint looks the same as one that's less than a day." Justin took a sip of his Coke, then set it down on a paper coaster Cameryn handed him.

She took a quick glance behind her to check her tables and saw Monica refreshing the water on the table with the kids. Relieved they couldn't overhear, Cameryn huddled closer again as Justin went on.

"After Brad slipped, Dwayne said Brad called him all the time for support, trying to keep himself sober. He was afraid if people found out he was drinking they might take Scouting away from him. I said to Dwayne, 'Why did you protect him when he was dead and it didn't matter anymore?' He told me that all Brad talked about was Scouting and teaching you kids. Dwayne didn't want to hurt the legacy."

"I'm assuming you checked all this out? With Alcoholics Anonymous?"

Justin sighed. He tapped the rim of his glass with his finger. "We're in the process. It's hard, because with A.A., everything's secret. They're not exactly a cooperative group."

"So you can't be sure of any of this."

"Cameryn, I'm sure. I talked to the man. He's devastated at the accusation, and he's got a good alibi for the night Brad died."

"Which is what?"

"He spent that night with his wife. They were trying to patch things up. I checked it out, and she was with him."

Lost in thought, Cameryn bit the side of her thumb. "If it's not Dwayne, we're back to having nothing."

"Worse than nothing," Justin told her. "So far, we can't make any connection fit. There was no motive to kill this man. Brad Oakes lived in this town for thirteen years, sober, kind, no problems with anyone. That leaves me with the most frightening scenario of all." His eyes bored into hers. "This might have been a random murder."

The thought scared her because she knew the challenge of finding someone who killed indiscriminately. Ninety-five percent of victims had a link to their killers, and part of forensics was to connect the dots back to the perpetrator. Boyfriend, neighbor, spouse, lover—those were the threads that law enforcement followed. But when there was no thread, no connection, the killer could slip away in anonymity. When the victim could be anyone, the killer could be anyone, too.

"Random killers almost never get caught," she murmured.

"Exactly. We still don't have a clue *how* the murder was done in the first place. We don't understand the mechanism. The sheriff called in the Colorado Bureau of Investigation, and they're reviewing the case now. You know what they told the sheriff?"

"What?"

"They said it's like some alien beamed him with a ray gun."

So intense was her concentration that she didn't notice the shape looming behind Justin's forward-leaning figure. When she finally focused beyond Justin's head she saw Kyle. His blond hair had been cut, almost buzzed, and stood straight up, stiff as spokes. His black snowboarding coat was stretched tightly across his chest. Seeing him was enough to wake her from her trance.

"Kyle, you're here!" she cried. For some reason she felt guilty. She sprang up and rounded the bar, holding out her arms. When he hugged her, his grip was iron.

"I was just talking to Justin about the case. There's a lot going on. Not anything I can tell you," she babbled, "but the case is just weird. So Justin was filling me in."

"I can see that. Hello, Officer Crowley." Kyle pulled one arm free from Cameryn and held it out to Justin. "Did you find out who's responsible?"

"Not yet." Justin's voice was cool. "We're still working on it."

"If there's anything I can do to help, let me know."

"I will." Justin stood and picked up the manila folder. "Well, I'd best be going. Thanks for the Coke, Cameryn. See you around."

"See you." She gave a tiny wave, and then he was gone, the bell on the door jingling behind him.

Kyle was scoping Cameryn's face. His eyes looked darker than before, almost as if the gold had disappeared. "What was that all about?" he asked.

"Nothing," Cameryn cried. "I was just working. He was talking to me about the case."

"Are you sure that's all?"

"Of course I'm sure!"

He put one palm on each of her cheeks and drew her close, resting his forehead against hers. His skin felt cool. "I can tell he likes you. I'm not sure I'm okay with him hanging around my girl."

"Woman." She felt the lightness return inside her, fizzing like Pop Rocks. "Kyle O'Neil, are you jealous?"

He gave her a slow grin.

"Well, are you?"

A beat later, and then, "Should I be?"

Before she had a chance to reply, she heard Monica chirp, "Hey Cammie—don't go yet! Wait!"

Cameryn pulled away from Kyle. She watched Monica slide forward as though she were skating to the bar rather than walking. Monica wore an already-dirty apron, and her hair, which had been braided, was coming undone. "I didn't know if you were still here. I'm glad

I checked—you got a phone call," she said. "Vanko took it in the back."

"Who is it?" Cameryn asked.

"I don't know. I think he said it's some lady named Hannah."

In an instant, Cameryn felt the blood drain from her face. It slid all the way to her chest, where it disappeared into the abyss of her stomach. Monica must not have noticed, because she chattered on.

"The lady said she needed to talk to you, but Vanko thought you'd already left, and then she got all upset because you were supposed to be working until six. She was asking for directions on how to get to the Grand. Vanko was trying to tell her, but his English isn't so good so I took it. I told her to hold on so I could check to see where you were. I'm glad you're still here 'cause the lady's already in Ouray."

In a dream, in a fog, Cameryn repeated, "Ouray?"

"Yeah. Which means"—Monica looked at her watch—"whoever she is, she's not far. She'll be here in about an hour. So come get the phone, Cammie. The lady is waiting."

Her mind numb, Cameryn gasped, "I . . . can't . . ." but Kyle broke in, "Show me where the phone is, Monica. I'll tell Hannah to come to my house—I'll give her directions. Cammie will meet her there."

Chapter Fifteen

KYLE'S HOUSE WAS a cabin high in the mountains. As he drove Cameryn up the winding dirt road, she tried to swallow down the hot broth of anxiety rising from her stomach. After fourteen years of separation, she would meet her mother in an hour, maybe two. Back at the Grand, after Kyle had given Hannah directions to his cabin, he'd hung up the phone and hugged Cameryn, reassuring her that everything would be okay.

"She sounds nice," he'd whispered into Cameryn's hair. He rocked while holding her in his arms, shifting his weight from foot to foot in a slow dance. "I'm so happy for you, Cammie."

But now, in his Subaru, she watched in panic as the dashboard clock nibbled away time. The glowing red numbers reconfigured her life while the last digit turned from four to five, another minute closer, and then from five to six. All she could think was: *I'm about to meet Hannah.* Unable to silence the cacophony of emotions, she felt her heart bursting with every beat until it hurt physically to breathe. Her hands gripped her knees so hard her fingers blanched white. Kyle seemed as nervous, too, because every few minutes he reached over to touch her.

"Thank you for letting me meet Hannah at your place," she said. "I didn't want to meet her where people knew me. I couldn't exactly meet her at my house, either."

"I told you I'd do anything to help. And my dad's on the road, so this will be completely private."

"Thanks," she said again, and then bit down on her cuticle so hard it began to bleed.

The road crisscrossed in switchbacks as they ascended, and Cameryn worried whether Hannah had a car that could make the climb. "My dad and I cut this road ourselves," Kyle told her. "It's not very wide, but it does the job. We have a chicken coop up there and a couple of goats. We had a horse a while back, but something ate it. A bear, we think."

But Cameryn wasn't listening. Instead, she looked at the evergreens marching toward her, their gnarled trunks visible at the base with their branches crossed as if in warning. *Stop!* they seemed to say. *Think this through!* For the hundredth time she wondered if she was doing the right thing.

"Nervous?" Kyle asked.

"Yes. Excited, too. And scared and terrified and everything else you can think of all mixed together. On top of all that, though, I guess I feel guilty."

"Guilty? Why guilty?"

"I feel guilty about not telling my dad. I keep thinking I should call him—"

"Don't do it! Don't tell him anything until *after* you've talked to Hannah." Kyle's voice was adamant. "Cammie, it's only fair to listen to what she has to say before you decide what's next. If your dad comes, then Hannah won't be able to tell you the truth. And that's what you want to get at, right? The truth?"

"Yes, that's what I want," she replied softly.

"I know it's not exactly the same, but this situation sort of reminds me of my dad. My mom never talked when my dad was around and then—boom—one day she left. Just out of the blue. I wish I could have heard what my mom really thought before she went away. But my dad ran things in our house, and I didn't want to go against him and then . . . it was too late."

"You know, you never talk about your dad, Kyle. What's he like?"

Kyle shrugged. "I don't know what to say. My dad's one to play his cards close to his chest. Except with his dog— he *loves* that animal. Last night he called and told me he fed Skooch a whole steak right in the motel room."

"Wow. He sounds nice."

"Except he's different with people. Like with Mr. Oakes—did I tell you my dad wanted me to drop out of Scouts because he decided Brad had too much influence over me?"

"No." Cameryn looked at him, her eyes wide. "When did that happen?"

"A while ago." Kyle's hands tightened on the wheel as he said, "That's just the point. I decided what *I* wanted to do, and that's what I did. That's what you should do with Hannah. See her by yourself, and then decide."

"You're right." Once again she was grateful to lie back in the current and let Kyle make the choice, because her mind was so thick with thoughts she couldn't sort them anymore. She would stay the course and see Hannah alone. The next bridge, the one where she told her father, would happen later. She'd cross it when she got there.

Kyle took a sharp right and pulled into a circle of dirt. Beyond it was a log house, two stories high with a steep-pitched green metal roof. The pathway led to a step up and then a wooden deck that wrapped around the house, and at the south end the ground dropped away to a small open field below.

"It's beautiful here," she breathed.

"If I'd known you were coming, I would have straightened up," he said, sheepish. "It's not too clean since we're a couple of bachelors now. Actually, it's mostly just me."

"It'll be perfect. Hannah won't care, and it'll be private."

"That's for sure. There's no one around for miles and miles."

The door was unlocked, and when she walked inside she realized Kyle had been correct; the house was not clean. It wasn't as messy as it was dirty. A film of dust covered everything, muting colors. There was a stack of newspapers yellowing in one corner, next to a huge fireplace, and beside that a pile of wood shedding bark. The fireplace wall was made of split rail. On it, high above, hung taxidermied animal heads watching her with glassy eyes. A deer with a huge rack, an elk, a moose, even a buffalo stared at her silently. Cameryn, who hated stuffed heads as a décor, asked, "Do you hunt?"

"Not me. My dad does. Me and my mom couldn't stand these things, so we took them down one week while my dad was gone trucking. You should have seen his face when he got back. He pitched a holy fit, and they've been up ever since. Do you want some water?"

"No thanks. Is that your father?" she asked, pointing to a picture on the wall. It was a photo of an aging cowboy, perched up high in his big rig. Grinning, he had one hand on an enormous steering wheel, the other draped over a dog sporting a bandana around its neck. The man's teeth were yellowed—cigarette-stained, she figured—and did not look well cared for. A straw cowboy hat had been wedged into the dash, its brim frayed. She never would have put this scrawny man together with Kyle; they seemed so opposite.

"Yeah, that's the old man. And his beloved dog. He won't be back for ten more days. Which is fine by me."

"Your dad doesn't look like you."

Kyle looked at her strangely, as though he was seeing, and yet not seeing her. Once, when her class had studied bald eagles, she'd learned that the birds possessed a protective inner eyelid, a thin membrane that covered the eye while the eagle tore into its prey. Back then, that was how she'd pictured Kyle. He, too, seemed to possess a kind of inner eyelid that obscured average kids from really registering in his line of sight. Seen, but not seen. That look, the one she'd forgotten, reappeared now as he turned back to his father's picture. All expression had drained from his face until it appeared almost blank.

"Thanks," he finally said. "I'm glad I don't look like Mr. Donny O'Neil. Actually, I look like my mother. She's a blonde, too." Running his hand over his mouth, he said, "You know, I wish I could do something useful. I'm feeling a little bit strange here, like *I'm* invading *your* space. Would you like me to leave?"

The truth was, she did want him to go. What was about to play out was so personal, so frightening, she didn't want any witnesses. Although she'd thought of a way, she wasn't sure it was all right to ask. Kyle had already done so much.

"I can see you're thinking," he said. "I see the wheels spinning. What is it?"

"I—I guess I didn't believe Hannah would be here so soon. I don't know, maybe I didn't think she'd actually come to Silverton at all. But the point is, she's almost here and I'm empty-handed."

"What do you mean?"

"I'm meeting my mom for the first time and I don't have anything to give her. I know it's kind of hokey, but I'd really like to give her some flowers."

A smile split across his face. "That's an awesome idea," he said. "Except I don't have any. I could run to town and get some roses."

"Not roses." Cameryn pictured the letter she'd received from Hannah, the one with the delicate watermark of an iris. "I'd like to give her irises. A huge armload of irises. But the only place that carries them is that specialty shop at Purgatory. That's a ways away and . . . is that too much to ask?"

"Not at all. I know which shop you mean. It's the one where the rich people go."

"Which means it'll cost a lot, I know. But I really want to do this. Do you think you could—?"

"Of course. I'll use my credit card."

"No," she protested, "I've got money—"

"Don't worry about it. I think I can make it there and back in forty minutes. An hour, tops. And the truth is, I don't mind having something to do." His keys jingled as he pulled them out of his pocket. Leaning over, he kissed her on the top of the head. "You sure you want me to go? Last chance to change your mind!"

"I think it might be best."

"All right. Help yourself to the refrigerator, although there's not much more than cold pizza. Bathroom's through that door over there, and the TV remote's on top of the coffee table. Let's see, you can go see my goats if you want—they're out in the pen. Just stay away from the chickens in that back coop. That's my dad's, and he doesn't like anyone out there."

"Not a problem."

"If you want to use my computer it's upstairs in my room. The desk over there is my dad's, so . . ."

"No worries. I won't touch it."

"Great. I'll be back in a flash."

With that, he was gone. As his car's taillights blinked through the trees, Cameryn realized how alone she was. Standing at the window, staring out, she looked at the pines and the darkening sky. A wind had kicked up, and she could hear the trees sigh as their tips swayed. The sound was mournful, like the organ at St. Patrick's. She felt pricks on her skin as she heard another sound: a rustling from the kitchen, and then she saw a reflected flash from behind her streak across the glass. As she whirled around, a dark shape leaped onto the top of the television, and a large, green-eyed gray cat stared at her, its whiskers drooping onto its paws.

"Good grief, cat, you about scared me to death. What's your name?"

The cat blinked. Stretching out a hind leg, it began to lick its paw.

If only she could be like that cat, she thought. No worries beyond yourself.

She began to pace. Below the mounted animal heads was a cuckoo clock, one that looked as though it had come from Germany. At the bottom of the pendulum swung a pinecone. She watched it click back and forth, counting the seconds. After that she got a glass of water and sipped it, but her stomach closed against it and she set it on the small rolltop desk. Then she wandered back to the picture.

Donny O'Neil had a wrinkled, weathered face and eyes that stared blankly at her from the photograph. Something nudged her mind, but she didn't know what. As she studied the picture she heard a crash, and turned just in time to see the cat lift its paws daintily over the water glass it had just knocked over on the desk.

"Dang it!" she cried. Racing into the kitchen, she grabbed some paper napkins and ran back to blot the water, which ran in a tiny waterfall between the slats of the rolltop. She could hear it drumming onto papers, like drops of rain. Rolling back the top, she saw it was worse than she thought. Papers were getting wet, ink smearing, edges curling—she picked them up and let the water pour off of them. Cursing under her breath, Cameryn realized that the napkins weren't enough, so she ran to the bathroom and grabbed a towel. Blotting, fanning, she tried to save as much as she could. It took her several moments to realize the paper she was holding was Kyle's, written in his square hand, and the teacher who had given the assignment, the teacher who had composed the comments scrawled in red across its top, was Mr. Oakes. The story was some sort of fiction; she could tell that much from skimming it. But it was the notes that caught her eye. She knew she shouldn't read them, but she couldn't resist. Mr. Oakes had inspired Kyle as a writer, after all.

This paper is technically masterful, and I feel it shows, as always, your intense ability. On that merit alone I have marked you an A.

Cameryn smiled, because Kyle was a straight-A student in all his classes. It made her proud to see his talent acknowledged by a teacher.

There is, however, a troubling disconnect between intellect and emotion in your work. You have structure, yes, but your protagonist is strangely cold throughout the prose.

In fact, all of your characters are without emotion alto-
gether. This is a story about death. Your writing would be
much deeper if you allowed yourself to plumb the depths.
Draw from your life, Kyle. You have your own tragic life
story concerning the death of your mother. Use that pain.
Writing can be cathartic, and I encourage you to release
the emotion inside on the safety of the printed page.

Cameryn's eyes widened. As she read the sentence
through again and again, her heart began to pound in
her ears. *The death of your mother!* Hadn't Kyle told her
his mother had left, just a few years before? And yet Mr.
Oakes was clearly addressing a death. It made no sense.
Why would Kyle lie? Especially to her?

Puzzled, she picked up another paper, and another,
carefully rifling through them for more written comments, but all she found were bills and letters addressed
to Donald O'Neil. There were no other papers of Kyle's.
She chewed her fingernail and read the comments again.
There it was, in black and white: *the death of your mother.*
Still there. It had not moved. It became clear to her that
Mr. Oakes had been mistaken. That was it—he'd tried to
help Kyle and he'd gotten it wrong. It was an odd mistake,
but mistakes happened. Or Kyle might have described
his mother's leaving as a death in and of itself. She nodded to herself. Yes, that could have been it. Having a
mother disappear was *like* a death, as she knew only
too well.

She shouldn't be snooping through the O'Neils' papers anyway. It was wrong. It got her thinking sideways, misinterpreting things. Blotting up the last of the water, Cameryn pulled down the rolltop and replaced the damp towel. Hannah was coming and she needed to prepare herself, to focus on that one all-consuming fact.

But it drummed in her mind: *Kyle lied to me.*

If his mother really was dead, there must be a reason he hadn't shared the story with her. She went to the couch, sat down, and crossed her legs. Maybe it had to do with his father, Donny. Maybe Donny had forbidden Kyle to tell the truth to anyone.

Her knee jiggled. Placing her hand on her knee to quiet it, she sat for as long as she could, then stood, realizing she would have to move or she would burst. It was dark outside—what if her mother missed the turnoff to this place? What then? Pacing, she went to the television, to the wall studded with heads, then wandered back to the picture. For some reason it drew her. There was something compelling in that picture, but whatever it was skittered along the edge of her consciousness. She stared at it again, searching it for . . . what?

Leaning so close her forehead almost touched the frame, she studied the photograph. Inside the truck cab were what she guessed to be wrappers and some empty cans. Her eyes focused on Donny's face, then back to the cab's interior. At the face, at the hat, then the dog.

The face, then the dog. Intense, she studied not the man, but the animal. It was a German shepherd. A German shepherd with a double notch in its ear. It was hard to see in the grainy photograph, but there it was, two slices that almost came to a point, like the letter *V.* Only a week before she'd seen another German shepherd with a notched ear, and with a start she realized that that dog's carcass from the side of the road had had the identical tan-and-black markings of the dog in the photograph. There was no doubt: *The dog in the picture and the dog left at the side of the road were one and the same! Donny had told his son the dog was eating steak, but this was the animal she'd seen dead on the road, which meant— Donny O'Neil was a liar!*

As her mind captured this fact, a chill crept down her skin, snaked inside her to pool in the pit of her stomach. *Brad Oakes. The dog. A man who lied to his son. A man who didn't like Mr. Oakes. Scorched tissue.* In her mind's eye she saw the same grayed flesh, the pewter-colored muscles, the same empty eye sockets. Her father had blamed the dog's missing eyes on scavenging animals, but what if he'd been wrong? What if there was another reason for the dog's bizarre condition? And what if it had something to do with Kyle's own father?

Hardly daring to even consider it, she imagined the possibility. If there was a link, there had to be a mechanism to bring it about—that explosion of the eyes and the cooking of the flesh without burns had to come from a real machine. If that was true, then a mechanism like that might still be here, in the O'Neil home.

No! She shook her head, hard. She was thinking crazy and she had to stop. But what if . . . ?

Cameryn looked at the picture and thought of calling Justin, but reconsidered when she realized what might happen if she did. Donny getting grilled by Sheriff Jacobs and Justin. Kyle's father would easily figure out the tip came from her. Maybe he'd tell Kyle he could never speak to her again! No, it was too risky. She couldn't gamble on evidence as tenuous as a spider's thread. There was only one way to answer her questions, and that was to find the answers herself. She'd look through this house to see if anything tied Donny back to Brad Oakes. Most important, she'd have to look for some kind of instrument that could destroy tissue. And she'd have to hurry.

Doing a swift mental calculation, she figured Kyle would be gone for maybe half an hour more, but her mother might arrive sooner. There wasn't much time.

Moving quickly, Cameryn began at the desk. Opening it once more, she hastily went through all the papers, not only the ones on the desktop but those inside the drawers, trying to disturb them as little as possible. Nothing. Next, she went to the kitchen, opening the cupboards, which were almost bare, aware that anything could be hidden anywhere and the safest thing to do was methodically check it all, inch by inch, room by room. The refrigerator, as Kyle had mentioned, was empty, save for the pizza box and a dozen eggs. She opened cabinets, checked beneath the sink, then returned to the living room and the hall closet. Inside were two coats and some heavy boots, a hat, and a box on a shelf. When she pulled down the box, it contained only gloves and some knit caps.

Faster now, she went up the stairs to Kyle's room. It was sparsely furnished, with a bed made smooth and tucked with hospital corners and a plain wooden desk with a Dell computer. Scouting manuals, schoolbooks, binders, wood carvings, a football trophy—things any normal kid would have. Relieved, she realized there was nothing.

Adrenaline surging, she went to the second room, Kyle's father's. A long, heavy flashlight, the kind that policemen carried, lay on the nightstand. A reading lamp had been left on, and there was a circle of light beneath it, like a halo. More careful now, she pulled open the drawer. Inside was a manila envelope, sent from the California Department of Health and Human Services. With trembling fingers, she opened it. Inside was a white sheet of paper, bordered in blue. The California state seal had been stamped in the bottom right-hand corner, and before she read it she knew what it was. A death cer-tificate. A death certificate with the name Sherrie O'Neil. Cause of death: gunshot wound to the head. Manner of death: suicide.

Stunned, she put the death certificate back into the drawer, her mind reeling. No wonder Kyle had lied to her. Nothing could be worse than death by suicide. Hannah had left Cameryn, that was true, but death—that was a permanent separation. What kind of secrets had been buried in this home? Could Donny O'Neil have killed his wife and covered it up? Could he have been killing all along?

She saw a photograph of Donny and Sherrie on the nightstand, their hands entwined. As she lifted the picture frame, guilt once again washed through her. What was she thinking? It must be the pressure of Hannah's arrival that was making Cameryn's thoughts so tangled. Her irrationality had allowed her to rifle through her boyfriend's house, and she was suddenly ashamed—the O'Neil family had gone through enough tragedy without her weaving theories out of wisps of fact. Cameryn knew she needed to pull her thoughts together, to focus on Hannah.

"I'm sorry," she whispered to the picture before setting it down. "I don't know what I'm doing. I must be losing my mind."

Donny stared back, silent, accusing. She was about to return to the couch and wait patiently for her mother when she looked again at the flashlight. Almost against her will, her mind began whirring once again. . . .

Just stay away from the chickens in that back coop. Those were his dad's orders, Kyle said. It was odd, really.

Why would Donny demand that? Biting her lip, she picked up the flashlight. Crazy, irrational, the accusations against herself pelted her mind, but one overriding thought was loudest of all. She knew if she didn't check that chicken coop, if she didn't answer this last question, she'd always wonder.

The flashlight was heavy, at least five pounds, but the shaft of light it made was twice as bright as any she had used before. Like a lighthouse beam, it cut through the darkness as she made her way to the one place he'd told her not to go.

Circling past a pen with two goats, she crossed to the wooden structure. Large for a coop, it looked more like an outbuilding, with the same green metal roof as the house. It had a fence around it, and feathers scattered against a crust of snow. She saw the stump of a felled tree, and on the stump, in a pool of dark blood, was an ax, its blade still embedded in the trunk. White feathers had made a mound at the base of the stump, blown by the wind like a miniature snowdrift. The gate squeaked as she opened it, and for a moment she thought the sound of it might scare the birds.

Then she realized a strange thing. There was no sound. Just the wind sighing overhead, whispering softly through the pine, lifting her hair and wrapping dark strands across her face. She pulled them away impatiently and put her hand on the metal knob. Pushing it open, she stepped inside.

It was dark, but with the flashlight she located a light switch and turned it on.

Planks had been nailed across one wall, dividing it like the score sheet of a tic-tac-toe board, but the coops were empty. Again, it didn't make sense. The dirt floors had been churned, and at the end of the building was a dog kennel and a workbench crammed with tools, tin cans, kerosene, saw blades. There was a smell in here that was hard to identify, making Cameryn raise her hand to her nose as she moved toward the workbench.

Since it was darker there, she kept the flashlight on. The beam danced across a myriad of tools, sharp and bright.

She saw a glass tube, a foot high. Next to that, a miniature rosebush whose petals had turned to dust. And the last items, set carefully along the workbench like curled fingers. They were ribs. Ribs that had been cleaned and dried and set carefully in place.

The ribs of a human.

Chapter Sixteen

HARDLY DARING TO breathe, Cameryn picked up the bones and held them high, examining them closely. They were curved and smooth to the touch, like ivory. At first she'd thought they were human, but on closer examination, she wasn't so sure. Pulling out her phone from her back pocket, she hit speed dial. A moment later, Dr. Moore's gruff voice answered.

"Hello?"

"Hi, Dr. Moore. It's me, Cameryn Mahoney."

"Are you aware what time it is?" he asked tartly. "It's long past business hours."

"Yes, I'm sorry to bother you," she said. "But this may be important."

"Your voice is shaking, Miss Mahoney. All you all right?"

"I don't know. I found some bones and I—I don't know what to think. I want to know if they're human. I'd like to send a picture over my phone to your computer. Could you please tell me what I'm looking at?"

There was a pause. "What kind of bones?"

"Ribs. They're just lying here, on a countertop, and I can't tell what kind they are."

"If you think they might be human, then I suggest you call the police."

"No!" she cried. And then, softer, "I can't do that. I don't want to start anything, not until I know."

Dr. Moore exhaled noisily. "Miss Mahoney, I'm going to have dinner with my wife. I'm already running late—"

"*Please,* Dr. Moore! Just a quick look," she begged. "I can send the picture right now. Please!"

She heard what sounded like the squeak of a chair. Then a deep sigh. "All right, send it now and I'll take a very quick look to appease you, and then we're done. You should be aware that I've got a life outside this office."

"Thank you, Dr. Moore!"

He gave his e-mail address, and Cameryn, with trembling hands, set down the bones and turned her phone to snap a picture. As soon as she sent it she asked, "Did you get it, Dr. Moore?"

"Not yet," he said. "For Pete's sake, give it a moment.

Young people are so impatient and they think everything's accomplished in an instant—oh, here it is. Now let me see. . . ."

As she waited for the answer, Cameryn felt her pulse thudding in her ears like a metronome set on high. Finally she blurted, "Can you tell anything?"

"Yes." Dr. Moore's tone was deep. "This is extremely serious."

"What? Are they human?"

"No. The truth is, Miss Mahoney, somebody had a barbeque and didn't invite you. These bones belong to a pig."

"A *pig*?"

"Yes. As in ribs for eating. As in the-secret's-in-the-sauce kind of barbecue ribs. You can tell because human ribs are thinner and have more of a curve, the articular facets are different, and they're not as tasty with a salt rub. As in you've just wasted my time and I'm late."

"Just one more thing," she begged humbly. "There's a plant here, a potted rose, I think, and its leaves have turned to dust."

"So now you think I'm a horticulturist?"

"I'm taking one more picture and sending it right now. I'm wondering if you've ever seen anything like it. There were a bunch of flowers next to Mr. Oakes's nightstand that withered just this same way."

"*Mmm*, here it is. I'm looking at flower dust. I'm not

an expert, but I have to say a great big 'so what?' Flowers wilt and crumble. Where are you, anyway?"

Relief flooded through her like a warm wave. These were pig bones, not human. Dr. Moore thought nothing of the flowers. She had been stupid and suspicious for no reason. Kyle would be here soon, her mother would come, and the pieces of her life would fall together smoothly. She'd almost blown it all because she'd let her imagination run wild.

"It doesn't matter," she said happily. "I was just having a 'senior moment'. As in senior-in-high-school moment." She felt light, giddy. "Everything's all right now. Go to your dinner. I really appreciate your help, and—"

"Wait."

It was the way he said that one word that made her breath stop again.

Dr. Moore barked, "Don't go just yet. I'm looking at the screen and—are you still near that flowerpot?"

"What?"

"Pay attention! Go back to the place where you took the picture of the flower petals."

"But you said flowers wilt and—"

"I'm not *talking* about the petals, Miss Mahoney. There's something in the background I want to get a better look at. That glass-and-metal tube. Do you see it? It's off camera a bit, behind the ribs and to the left. Take a full picture of it and send it to me."

"But why? I thought you said—"

"Just do it. There's a word on the bottom of the tube, a label—I can only get a partial read. Right now I see an 'i' and an 'a' and an 'n'. Turn it so I can get the whole word."

Cameryn looked down on the bench and saw blue letters, silk-screened on the black metal part of the tube. "Yes," she said. "I have it."

"Photograph it, then send it to me. I want the entire name to be in the picture."

She turned the base of the glass tube and snapped another photo, this one including the word "Virian." After she forwarded it to Dr. Moore she asked, "What are you looking for?"

"Let me be . . . sure. It may be nothing. Did I ever tell you I was in the army? Vietnam . . . Working in military research and . . . Ah, here it is, it just arrived. Now give me a moment. . . ."

The tube, as Cameryn looked at it, didn't seem like much. Just a thin glass dome with wires inside, the end screwed into a metal base with leads coming out the side. Then she saw something else: next to the tube were three black squares connected with cables. They were some sort of power supply. As she fingered the cables, she heard Dr. Moore's voice bark in her ear.

"Cameryn!"

The way he said her name made her jump. "What?"

"Where are you?"

"I'm in a chicken coop—"

Dr. Moore's voice had ratcheted up. "I want you to get out of there. *Right now!* Drop whatever it is you're doing and go. What you've got there is a klystron tube—"

It took a moment for Cameryn to register this. "A what?"

"A klystron tube!" he shouted. "Don't question me, just do what I say!"

"I don't understand—"

"I saw klystrons when I was in the army. Those things emit enough radiation to microwave a human being in less than three minutes! It would cook a man in his own bed!"

Cameryn's hand recoiled from the thin, clear glass. "This thing is a *microwave?*" She thought of the seared flesh, the cooked muscles, the eyes that would explode when the long waves hit the liquid in their orbs. "Oh my God!" she cried. "This is what killed Mr. Oakes!"

"I don't know why I didn't think of it at the autopsy. That tube is a ten-thousand-watt microwave! A microwave that can go straight through a wall and cook someone in their bed. It fits the nature of his death precisely and I—where are you?" He was shouting now. "Listen to me—*wherever you are, get out of there immediately and—*"

"I'll take that," a voice said. Quick as lightning, a hand, Kyle's hand, reached in front of her and snatched the phone from her, snapping it shut with a small click.

Whirling around, she saw irises scattered in a blanket of purple, their green stalks strewn like Pick-Up Sticks across the floor. Kyle was staring at her, his handsome face distorted with an expression she'd never seen before.

"Kyle! What are you—what are you doing here?" she stammered. Her mind, which had been frenetically spinning, froze.

"I was just about to ask you the same thing." He looked at her, his face realigning itself so that he looked like himself again. But his voice was distant, cold. "I can't believe you disobeyed me, Cameryn. I said you could go anywhere in my house except for one place. I asked you to stay out of my chicken coop. What part of that didn't you understand?"

"*Your* chicken coop? Then . . . it's not your father's?"

"I told you that, didn't I? No, this place is mine."

She had been so desperate to believe that Donny was the killer. Not Kyle. Never Kyle! But hope began to die as she looked into his eyes. The golden flecks had turned to ice.

Waving his hand expansively, he said, "This is my own special place. It's off-limits—even my dad doesn't come in. The coop is where I do my . . . experiments. And here I find you inside, snooping." A beat, and then, "Who were you talking to?"

Trying to keep her voice even, she said, "Come on, Kyle, give me my phone. This isn't funny."

"I'm not trying to be. I have to say I'm disappointed in you, Cameryn. When I realized you worked with the dead, well, I thought you were different. More like me." He sighed. "But I guess you're just like everyone else." Stuffing the cell phone into his back pocket, he stepped closer. "People always let me down. My mom. My dad. Mr. Oakes." Suddenly, he became quiet. He stared at her, blinking. "And now you."

There were too many thoughts to make sense of any of them. Kyle had burst into her life and she'd let herself go, but none of it had been real. Or was it? Who was the person standing before her? There was the mouth that had kissed her, the hands that had held her, but that person had been nothing more than shadow. How could she have been so wrong? She wanted to give in to her fear, but she knew she couldn't. Right now, she had to survive.

"Okay," she said, forcing a smile. "You got me. I shouldn't have come in here, but I thought I heard something and I came to check, and—I need to go, Kyle. I have to go home now."

"But I don't want you to leave," he told her. His voice shifted ever so slightly. It became darker, his tone deepening as though he possessed some otherworldly authority. "You *have* to stay. Besides, I don't know why you think you're going anywhere."

"Kyle—"

"Don't blame me. You did this to yourself."

He took a step closer, his finger lightly caressing her cheek, but Cameryn recoiled from his touch. It was as if she could see inside him, and as she did she realized what Kyle was—not a man, not an animal, but something in between. The mask had slipped and she could see inside. He had used the klystron tube to kill their teacher. Worse, he knew she knew. Her heart began to beat wildly as fear enfolded her. She was alone on a mountain with a murderer. Not the father but the son.

"Are you afraid, Cammie?" He took a step toward her. "I know you're afraid. I have a sixth sense. It's strange—I can almost smell it when people are full of fear."

She raised her arm to hit him, but he caught her arms, clasping both her wrists in one hand as he took something from his belt. The blade caught the light, glittering. Cameryn's heart froze as she tried to comprehend that Kyle O'Neil had a knife and there was nothing she could do, nowhere she could go, no way to save herself.

"Don't fight me. You'll only make it worse." Everything in his face was dead except his eyes. They were fixed on Cameryn's with an intensity she'd never seen before, like a magnifying glass burning into her soul. Apart from his eyes, his face was so still it was as though it were embalmed.

"If you hadn't come in here, I would never have hurt you. Now everything's . . . complicated."

There was nothing she could say to this. She pulled against him, but his grip was like steel. With his left hand he foraged along the table, grasping a roll of duct tape, then slipping it onto his wrist like a bracelet. Next he reached for a dusty chair and banged it onto the floor.

"Sit!" he commanded.

The knife curved at the end, as though it was grinning. "Put your hands behind your back. Do it!" The tip of the blade grazed against her throat. All she could do was follow his orders. He pulled her shaking hands behind the back of the chair and wrapped duct tape around her wrists, looping it again and again. Cameryn knew about duct tape. Criminals used it all the time because there was no way to break the bond. Binding her ankles, he then looped the tape around a chair leg and up through the handles of a large cabinet behind her. All the while he kept up his diatribe against her.

"What happens to you now is not my fault," he kept saying over and over, ignoring her pleas of "Why?"

She knew then that he was going to kill her. She was a witness, and she'd seen his instrument of death. Using a klystron tube, Kyle had murdered his teacher, the one who he said inspired his writing. He had kissed Cameryn and lied to her face, and now she was in the wilderness, far away from anyone who could help her.

The outbuilding had a single window facing away from the house. Looking out, she could see a patch of stars. But then she saw something else—a reflected light approaching, beams from a car's headlights, she guessed. She heard the crunch of tires on the dirt and rocks, and an engine turning off and a door slamming, and footsteps, faltering as they approached Kyle's house.

Leaning in close, Kyle whispered into her ear, and she felt his hot breath inside her, as though he himself could enter her mind. "Don't say a word," he said softly.

Tears welled in her eyes as she nodded silently. She strained to hear. For a moment there was nothing but silence, and then a pounding on the door. More silence, and then a light, wavering voice called out. "Cameryn, are you there?" Another pause, and then, "It's me, Hannah."

The tip of the knife pressed against her windpipe. "Shhhhh," he murmured.

"I've come a long way to see you," the voice cried. "I know it's hard but—if you're in there, please, come to the door."

Her mother, whom she couldn't remember, was only forty feet away. Cameryn was going to die, and her mother would never know how much Cameryn had wanted to see her, to hear her in person and touch her face.

"Please, open the door." The pounding was harder, five strikes with her fist, and then Cameryn heard a choked sob.

"Please!"

"Please," Cameryn echoed in the barest whisper. But Kyle merely pressed the blade more deeply in reply. She could feel her skin give way to the tip, felt the bite of it, and the warm trickle of blood, no wider than a pencil, snaking down her neck.

"See what you made me do?" Kyle hissed.

And outside, Hannah's anguished voice. "What's happened? Why won't you come out to me?" The next words she said were muffled, something Cameryn could not make out. And then, "I'll leave, if that's what you want."

"It's what you want," Kyle whispered into Cameryn's ear.

And then what Cameryn wanted most and dreaded most happened at the same moment. Her mother got back into the car. The door slammed, the engine coughed, and the car and the lights disappeared down the mountain in a burst of gravel. Cameryn felt the invisible cord between them, the one she had put her hopes on, stretch and then break. But at least Hannah was safe.

"It's just the two of us now," Kyle said, straightening. "That must have been hard. You waited all your life for that moment, only to miss it. Too bad."

"What is *wrong* with you?" Cameryn cried.

Different expressions flitted across his face until he finally settled on one—amusement. "It depends on who you ask. Now, Brad Oakes—he read my writing, and you know what he thought? He said I had—wait, how did he put it?—an attachment disorder. When I fried my dad's dog I didn't feel anything. So I guess Brad Oakes was right. I'm not like everyone else. In my world, that's a good thing."

Cameryn's tongue felt too thick for her mouth, or maybe it was her throat tightening so that she could hardly breathe. Her heart, her thoughts, pounded inside her. "Is that why you killed Mr. Oakes?" she croaked. "Because he knew what you were?"

"Ah, the million-dollar question. Why. It's not what you think." He walked over and pushed the klystron tube to the edge of the workbench, directly in front of Cameryn. Slowly, deliberately, he plugged the cables into the tube, as though he had all the time in the world. "Have you ever heard of Leopold and Loeb? Thomas Koskovich and Jayson Vreeland? Or maybe Jon Venables and Robert Thompson, who killed a little boy when the two of them were only ten years old. It's amazing, when you think about it. They started killing at *ten* years of age. Why? For what reason? They just wanted to see what it felt like to take a life."

"Kyle—"

"Maybe you've heard of Gary Hirte. He's another Eagle Scout like me, who killed just to see if he could do it and get away with it. We are a group of very special human beings. A small, *exclusive* group."

"You think being able to kill makes you *special*?"

Kyle looked at her, his hazel eyes impassive. "I'm in control. Of who lives, who dies. That kind of power is addictive. I hinted that Brad and Dwayne were, how shall I put it, closer than friends, and watched everyone scramble after my lead. It's the ultimate high." He paused, then said, "Could you do it? Could you kill someone, Cameryn?"

"Of course not!"

That smile again, curling up the corner of his lip. "If you could get free, I imagine you'd try to kill me. I'm trying to explain this to you. We, those who are like me, we kill because we want to. It's the ultimate game, really. Can I commit the perfect murder and not get caught? Eagle Scout Gary Hirte made a fatal mistake—he kept the knife he used for the kill inside its still-bloody sheath. The victim's DNA was right there, in Gary's own bedroom, linking him directly to his crime. Stupid, and sloppy." Kyle shook his head. "An Eagle Scout ought to be smarter than that."

He was intent now, absorbed in the fifteen-inch glass tube. "So in my research on microwaves, I stumbled on the ultimate killing machine. A klystron is used in high-power, high-frequency radio transmitters." Shrugging, he said, "The terminology's not important. I want you to understand—*no one* has ever used a klystron to commit a murder before this. *I* put it all together. Me. Kyle O'Neil. You found the bones of our pig. I put him in the dog carrier and practiced training the beam on him. I was amazed when it worked. He squealed a lot, though. Fortunately, no one could hear him way up here. I dissected him to examine the results." Kyle paused. "Do you know what makes this method so special?"

Cameryn sat like stone.

"I killed Brad Oakes from the *outside* of his house. That's the pure genius of it. I didn't leave a trace inside the crime scene. Not a hair. Not a fiber. I plugged the klystron into an outside outlet, aimed it, and"—he snapped his fingers—"that was the end of the man."

Barely squeezing out the words, she asked, "Why Mr. Oakes?"

"Because I'm merciful. I picked him because his last living relative died. He had no family. I chose someone who would hardly be missed." He turned to look at her. Reaching out, he stroked her hair. Cameryn jerked away. "I want you to know, you made the experience more special, Cammie. I want to thank you for that."

Behind her, she pulled her wrists as hard as she could, but the duct tape held like handcuffs. Her flesh ripped against it, pain shot up her arms, and the tape held fast.

"You'll never break the tape, Cammie, but good for you for trying. Yes, you made it even better. You were like a bonus, like extra credit points. Part of the fun is watching the police and the forensic team trying to figure out what happened. I mean, they were *idiots*! They had *no idea*!" He laughed, hollowly. "You were my conduit, my eyes into what they were thinking. It was awesome, talking to you about the case. I got to relive it over and over." He closed his eyes, a look of pure pleasure on his face.

Cameryn understood a terrible fact: to destroy the single witness, he would have to destroy her. There was nothing she could do. The books said a victim should keep the perpetrator talking in order to personalize themselves, but even as the strategy raced through her mind she knew how futile it was. Kyle had known Brad Oakes well. He killed him, just the same.

"Kyle," she said, pleading, "I don't think you really want to hurt me. I think you don't really want to do this."

Not seeming to hear, he took the plug and pushed it into the outlet. "You want to know why people like me do what we do? That answer is simple. We kill," he said, "because we can. Besides, murder isn't that bad. We all gotta die sometime. Mortality stands at one hundred percent."

"Please!" she cried.

He turned back to the tube, his hand on more cables.

"I know about your mother!"

Kyle whipped around. The smile, so obvious before,

melted from his face. Anger rose in its place, coloring his cheeks, igniting his eyes.

"I know what happened to her! I saw the death certificate! Did you kill her? I actually thought it might have been your dad, but now I think it was you! You killed her, didn't you?"

He stood, frozen. The cables slipped through his hands as he hissed, "Shut up."

But Cameryn couldn't stop. She'd managed to penetrate his shield, to puncture his veneer. "Why did you do it?"

"I said, shut *up!*" With the back of his hand he smacked her on the side of the head, and for a moment her vision exploded in stars. "I would never hurt my mother," he cried. "*She* left *me!* I would never, *ever* hurt her. Shut up, shut up, shut *up!*"

Quietly, Cameryn said, "She left you by putting a bullet in her brain."

Kyle raised his arm to strike again, but then, thinking better of it, he clenched his fist and lowered it to his side. He was breathing rapidly, panting.

"My mom left me, too, Kyle," Cameryn said. "But she came back. And she's out there, waiting for me." Tears blurred her vision, but she could see him standing there, riveted by her words. "They already know I was with you tonight. If you hurt me they'll know it's you. You've got nothing to gain anymore."

"You don't know anything!"

"I know that you're a human being. I saw inside you, Kyle. Let me have a chance with *my* mother. Let me have a chance to live. Please, Kyle. *Anam cara.*"

Kyle looked up at the ceiling and took a deep breath. How much real time went by was hard to say, but to Cameryn it had suspended into another dimension. The pounding of her heart and the throbbing from the prick of the knife were her only clues that it was seconds, not hours, that passed. When she saw him reach for the tube she knew she had lost. But he didn't turn it on. Instead, he skimmed past it to grab the roll of duct tape. Ripping a smaller piece, cutting it with his teeth, he pressed it over her mouth. Then he turned and walked toward the door.

"I'm an Eagle Scout. I can survive in the wilderness or wherever I choose. I'm going to give you two guarantees: One, they'll never, ever find me. And two"—he held up his middle and index fingers, pressed together in a salute—"one day, when you least expect it, I'll be back." He looked around the barn, his hand on the light switch. "You're like me, Cameryn. More than you know." Opening the door, he pulled his collar tight, looking at the sky. "Wow, it's cold out here—freezing, actually—and you've got no coat. But still, I'm giving you a chance. If it's meant to be, you'll live. If you live, you can tell my story. *Anam cara.*"

With that, he flicked off the light and slammed the door shut, leaving her in total darkness. She heard the latch slide in place. And then he was gone.

Chapter Seventeen

IT WAS DARK inside the chicken coop, and the cold was beginning to seep into Cameryn's bones. If she turned her head and strained, she could see bits of starlight through the corner of the window, could hear the trees moaning in lament, could feel the shiver of a breeze as it pushed through the small opening where the chickens, when they were alive, must have pecked and scratched. This remote mountain lay blanketed in a silence like nothing she'd ever experienced before. As her terror over Kyle subsided, a new fear took its place. She realized she was completely and utterly alone.

Her neck throbbed. She could tell the bleeding had stopped, because the dried blood tugged against her skin whenever she moved her head. In the bit of light, she made out the shape of the pig ribs, curved and grinning, lying near the base of the klystron tube. A mentality that could murder animals and humans for sport was totally twisted and abhorrent: Kyle said he killed because he was special, as if emotion was a weakness he was blessed to live without.

Something scraped against the metal roof, the noise magnified in the stillness. Fear stabbed her heart—was Kyle still out there, hovering in the woods, playing an insane game with her? There was no doubt he could change his mind and return to finish the job. Leave no witness. Strip the flesh off her bones like he had the pig. Her pulse pounded in her neck as she strained to see.

More scraping, then a sound of fingers drumming against metal. *Kyle!* Adrenaline shot through her until she realized that it was only branches chafing against the roof. *Stay calm,* she commanded. *You're hyperventilating. You'll lose body heat too fast. That's it—nice and easy.*

Time slowed to a nauseating crawl as her fingers began to quiver and then finally go numb. Straining against the tape was futile, but she did it anyway until her muscles burned. It was hard to control her emotions. Every night sound became sinister: The squeak of a gate might be Kyle at the door, sliding back the lock; the howl of the wind was Kyle at the window, watching her. Inanimate objects were suddenly malevolent and alive. To cope, she forced herself to make lists of people who would miss her, of steps they would take to find her. But it was possible that no one would begin to put the pieces together until morning, and by then it could be too late.

Her father didn't know where she was. No one did, except . . . one person. And she might be driving back to New York by now, certain her daughter didn't want her. Cameryn wept at the thought of it. She tried to scream in fear and frustration, but the sound was muffled, high-pitched, and thin, and what was the point of it? No one would hear her.

Think, don't panic! she commanded herself. There *had* to be a way out. With all her strength she pitched forward, but the cabinet Kyle had tied her to tipped against her back, threatening to crush her. The cabinet was free-standing and heavy. She wondered if she could manage the weight and pull it, and herself, to the door. Heaving forward again, she heard something inside slam against the metal doors, then felt the weight of it push her chest against her thighs, trapping her, squeezing the air out of her lungs. It couldn't work! Fighting for breath, she heaved backward with every bit of her strength, her neck pulsing and probably bleeding again, until the cabinet finally righted itself against the wall with a bang. Kyle had known exactly what he was doing. She was helpless.

Think! she ordered herself again. *Assess the facts. I can make it without water, but the mountains at night are freezing. Bodies can only cool off a few degrees before going into hypothermia. In this temperature I could lose a degree every couple of hours, so if I'm here all night . . .* She longed for her coat—why hadn't she worn it? Then her mind shifted once again to Hannah, driving away, and she grieved for what her mother must be thinking: that her only daughter hadn't cared, an abandonment in reverse. And her father . . .

As the darkness pressed in and the coldness wrapped around Cameryn's flesh, she came to realize something more. The sins of her father seemed so much smaller now. There was a clarity that hadn't been there before, as though she could see her life on a screen. Her father had tried to protect her—wrongly, maybe—but he only wanted to shield her from hurt, and in return she'd hidden from him. When she got out of here, *if* she got out, things would be different. With her mammaw, too. Her mammaw, who'd sought to replace her mother.

I'm sorry, she thought. *I'm so sorry.*

As time passed, Cameryn felt her extremities slowly turn to wood. The moon's pale light pulled away from the window, and every minute became colder and darker, inside as well as out. How long had she been here? Two, maybe three hours. She guessed it was past ten o'clock, but she had no way to know for sure. Her father wouldn't even realize she was gone, not yet. She was shivering, and she couldn't stop it, her body's futile way of generating heat.

Suddenly she saw a light bouncing off the scaffolding of the branches, and she felt a surge of joy. Followed by fear. Joy, that someone was coming for her; fear that the someone was Kyle. Had he returned? He was smart, and killing her was the intelligent thing to do. Yet, inexplicably, he had spared her. Until now. Panic welled inside as she realized that the car door slamming like a gunshot could be Kyle's, that the feet scuffing up the steps might be . . .

Someone pounded on the front door of Kyle's house. It wasn't Kyle! Kyle wouldn't do that at his own home! Cameryn knew she had to signal whoever it was before they turned and drove away, as Hannah had. Slamming her back into the cabinet as hard as she could, she made the metal drawers boom like kettle drums. Her nostrils flared as she labored to breathe, tried futilely to cry out, banging the cabinet to signal whoever was out there. Over her drumbeat she couldn't hear the footsteps coming or the creak of the door handle, but she stopped cold when she saw the door open. A hand, white and gleaming, fumbled for the light switch, and then light flooded her eyes, burning them, and she had to squeeze them shut, but not before she saw her rescuer.

Lyric!

Blue hair streaming, her arms outstretched, Lyric cried, "Oh my God, Cammie! Oh my God! Hold still! Let me cut you free."

Red-and-blue lights flashed from the top of Justin's squad car, illuminating the pines around them like a mirrored disco ball. Cameryn, now wrapped tightly in a blanket, stood with Lyric on the porch. She stared into the dark trees and shivered.

"Aren't you cold?" Lyric asked. "Your skin was like ice, and now you're barely warmed up and you're back out here. Don't you think you should go inside?"

"They're going to seal it off as a crime scene. I'm *fine*, Lyric. Jacobs wanted to call an ambulance, but I showed him my fingers and toes. He's convinced I'm okay. He's a paramedic, you know."

"Why don't you let me take you home?"

"I will, after Jacobs talks to me. He's in the chicken coop with Justin and—I'm okay," she said. "Really."

The porch light flooded the deck, making the night sky almost impossible to see, but Cameryn knew the stars were out there just beyond her sight, twinkling silently in their heaven. Everything on the porch became outlined by the stark glare: the wooden railing, the empty flower boxes, and most important, Lyric's hair, the color of lapis lazuli. Lyric, in her thick, down-filled coat, stood like a rock beside her. *The* rock—Cameryn's rock. She'd pushed her away, but Lyric had come back.

Beneath the blanket, Cameryn's heart was still beating like a hammer as she tried to make sense of things that made no sense. It was as though she'd been on a journey out to sea in a small, ragged dinghy, and she'd made it home again.

"Your dad's probably driving like a bat out of hell from Ouray," Lyric said.

"Yes, I told him to go slow, but he sounded pretty scared." Cameryn gathered the blanket tightly around her neck. She must have winced in doing so, because Lyric put her arm around her and pulled her into her soft torso, asking, "Does your neck hurt?"

"It's not too bad. It was just a prick."

Lyric's voice became suddenly hard. "It's more than a prick—Kyle was out of his freakin' mind. You could have died in there!"

"I know it," Cameryn answered softly. "But the thing is, he wasn't out of his mind. He wasn't crazy. I . . . I think I would have been less afraid if he was." She began to shiver again, as hard as she had before, and even with her coat and the layer of blanket, she didn't know if she could stop. "I was so stupid, Lyric. I can't believe I was so incredibly *stupid*." Tears welled up, blurring the wooden boxes with their withered flowers, the brown stalks brittle and dead. "Everything he told me was a lie. The person I cared about didn't even exist."

"He fooled everyone. You're safe now," Lyric told her gently. Crescent moons swung from her ears as her ring-studded fingers rubbed Cameryn's arms. "You've had a trauma that would have put me in bed for weeks, but you're still here, still standing. You're safe," she said again.

The door to the outbuilding slammed, and Cameryn watched Sheriff Jacobs and Justin emerge. The sheriff had on a cap with actual earmuffs flapping against the side of his face like dog's ears, which Cameryn would have laughed at if this had been any other time. Justin, though, seemed filled with apprehension. Even from a distance, Cameryn could tell he wanted to come to her, to be near enough to be sure she was truly all right. He'd wanted to be with her from the start, but Sheriff Jacobs had insisted they go and check the klystron tube. Always the good deputy, Justin had followed his boss, but he'd left a trail of significant looks behind. And now he was back again, his eyes boring into hers, talking to her without words.

The sheriff's boots clumped up the wooden steps. "Well, Angel of Death, it looks like you received a miracle tonight," he said. "If Kyle woulda thrown that switch, you'd have fried."

"Don't call her that, sir," Justin said. "She doesn't like it."

The sheriff paused, turning toward Justin. Then he grinned. "Oh she doesn't, does she?"

Justin thrust out his chin. "No, sir."

Sheriff Jacobs turned again to look straight at Cameryn.

"Well," he said, "I meant no harm. Actually, the real Angel of Death was Kyle O'Neil. We opened that cupboard, the one he taped you to. It was chock-full of animal bones. Looks like he'd been cookin' up critters for a while. Got the tube right off eBay, if you can believe that. Fifty bucks."

Cameryn stayed speechless.

"They say the crazies always start with animals, and intellectually, I knew that," Jacobs continued. "Still, I'm telling you, it was pretty hard to see what Kyle'd done. There were at least five cats in there, plus what looked to be a couple of dogs and a bunch of chickens and Lord knows what-all. He's one of the sickest sons of—"

"What about his father?" Cameryn interrupted. Concern for Donny O'Neil had been playing like a bass note in the back of her mind.

"He's alive, if that's what you're asking. He's been picked up by the Tennessee cops. It's still sketchy, but Donny told 'em that it'd be hard to find his son if he wants to stay hid. That part worries me—that boy is as dangerous as a Jeffrey Dahmer. In fact, I changed my mind. He's not the Angel of Death. He's the Devil himself."

Justin came to Cameryn and put his hand on her shoulder. He squeezed, just once, but Cameryn felt his warmth spread through her. The sheriff looked at them sharply, then cleared his throat.

"I, uh, owe you two kids an apology. Looks like Kyle

actually microwaved his daddy's dog. You two spotted it, but I didn't believe there was a connection. I missed an important clue."

"It's hard to imagine anyone as twisted as Kyle," Cameryn answered softly.

"That's what's so scary about Kyle and his kind," said Jacobs. "That boy's got all the signs of a sociopath. Sociopaths don't really even *have* emotions. They don't feel. They watch other people and mimic things, but it's all acting. It's like they're not real human beings."

"He let me live," Cameryn said.

"That's true. But he probably thought you would die." Jacobs pulled on his long nose. "All of this is speculation, anyway—I haven't even talked to him yet. Or Donny."

Lyric dropped her arm from Cameryn's sleeve. Her face was working itself up into an expression Cameryn knew all too well: she'd heard the facts but they made little sense. Her brow furrowed, and her kohl-rimmed eyes narrowed as she spoke. "Sheriff," she said, "can I ask you something?"

"Shoot."

"Why couldn't we tell? I mean, we—me and Cammie—we went to school with Kyle. He sat right beside us. We saw him every day. How could he have fooled us?"

Before he answered, Jacobs pulled off his hat and held it between his hands. The thin hair on his head stood in swirls, like unraveled threads, as he scratched it. "I'm not sure I can really explain it, Lyric, except to say some people are chameleons. They know how to become whatever they figure folks want them to be." He took a deep breath and stated, "If he's what I think he is, then him and his breed are the most frightening people on our planet."

The four of them fell silent then. Sheriff Jacobs put his hand on the railing, his face impassive in the glare of the blue-and-red flashes. Wind shivered the pines, making them drop needles like flakes of snow as he said slowly, "The idea that he's out there terrifies me. I gotta hope we find him soon. There's no doubt in my mind he'll kill again." His glasses winked in the lights as he took them off and dropped them into his coat pocket. "Cammie, you already talked about Kyle letting you go, but I doubt you understand how truly lucky you are. Why he didn't kill you when he had the chance baffles me. That kid wasn't one to show mercy—a look in that cupboard tells the story. It's amazing, truly amazing, that he left you alive."

"He said if I was *meant* to live, I would."

"I say you're one lucky lady."

Taking a step forward, Justin said, "I'd like to ask Cameryn a couple of questions. Would that be all right, sir?" He looked from Lyric to the sheriff, who, nodding, rubbed his chin.

"I think I can allow you to interrogate this witness," Jacobs said. "For a few minutes, at least. Lyric, I have a couple of questions for you myself. We'll have to sit in my squad car. The Durango cops are on their way."

"Oh," Lyric said. "Right." She gave Cameryn's hand a quick squeeze and followed the sheriff, and suddenly Cameryn and Justin were alone. He moved to stand in front of her, looking down into her eyes. The light behind him made his face hard to read, but there was no mistaking his voice.

"Cammie," he said. His tone was husky. "When I heard what happened I almost went crazy. I should have known. In my gut, I always thought there was something off about Kyle, but I never thought he was capable of this."

"Neither did I."

The wind was moving his hair across his eyes, but Justin left it. "I've got to tell you, I was in a panic when Dr. Moore called us. Problem was, the sheriff and I didn't know where to start looking. Your pop's cell phone was out of area, your mammaw wasn't home—we didn't know where to start." Justin's voice shook a little. "It's so lucky Hannah called Lyric."

"The day we found Mr. Oakes," Cameryn explained, "Lyric told Hannah to call her if she ever couldn't reach me. The irony was that tonight, Lyric came here because Hannah told her I wouldn't even answer the door. Lyric thought Kyle had put me up to it, and that made her mad—she came here to yell at me. You're right. I've been lucky."

"It's been a night of second chances. For you, for me,

and . . ." Justin put his hand on her shoulder, pressing gently. "For Hannah."

Her heart stopped. "What are you saying?" she whispered hoarsely.

"She's here, tonight. Hannah came back."

"Where is she?"

He didn't say a word. Instead, his eyes flicked to the hand-cut road beneath them. There, just beyond the squad car, stood a woman. Like a spirit, the form was barely visible, a flash of white that was the face, two moving slashes that were her legs. The closer she came, the more the shape materialized. The woman was small—the same size as Cameryn—and thin. Cameryn strained to see, and as the woman took two steps closer, she saw the same dark hair curling past her shoulders, the same gait in her step.

"She came back," Cameryn breathed.

"Are you ready to meet her?"

It took only a moment for Cameryn to nod her head. She pulled away from Justin and gazed into the darkness. Tears blurred her eyes as she saw the woman take another tentative step toward the light. The wind howled as Cameryn leaped from the porch onto the uneven dirt road and started to run. And now Hannah was running, too, crying out Cameryn's name, her arms flung wide. Hardly daring to believe, Cameryn hurled herself forward, into the thin, strong arms.

The arms of her mother.

Acknowledgments

I'd like to thank the many people who helped me explore the forensic field. You have unselfishly shared your knowledge and passion—the glimpse into your world rocked mine! I'm especially grateful to: Thomas M. Canfield, MD, Fellow at the American Academy of Forensic Sciences, Chief Medical Examiner, Office of Medical Investigations; Kristina Maxfield, Coroner; Robert C. Bux, MD, Coroner, Medical Examiner, Forensic Pathologist; David L. Bowerman, Coroner, Forensic Pathologist; Dawn Miller, Deputy Coroner; Werner Jenkins, Chief Forensic Toxicologist; Chris Clarke, Forensic Toxicologist; Sandy Way, Administrator, El Paso County Coroner's Office; Sheriff Sue Kurtz, San Juan County Sheriff's Office; Melody Skinner, Administrative Assistant, San Juan County Sheriff's Office; Thomas Carr, Archeologist, Colorado Historical Society; and a special thanks to Robert Scott Mackey, D-ABMDI Deputy Coroner—an inspiriting professional and my conduit into a macabre world.

Alane Ferguson is the author of *The Christopher Killer*—the first book about Cameryn Mahoney—as well as numerous novels and mysteries, including the Edgar Award–winning *Show Me the Evidence*. She does intensive research for her books, attending autopsies and interviewing forensic pathologists as she delves into the fascinating world of medical examiners.

Ms. Ferguson lives with her husband Ron near the foothills of the Colorado Rockies. For more information about Ms. Ferguson and her books, please visit www.alaneferguson.com.